Hello readers!

Bury My Body Somewhere Nice: A Collection of Dark Stories is exactly that. It is a collection of five short stories that deal with some pretty dark themes. You can find content warnings on the very last page of this book, by visiting www.kalvinellis.com, or by scanning the QR code above.

Acknowledgment and Dedication

When I was ten years old I was afraid. By that young age I'd been through a lot of things no kid should ever have to go through. My escape from the horror that was life was found in movies and books. My mom had married a man who owned a small independent video store that happened to be next door to a used book store. Any time my step-dad needed his office I would have to pause whatever movie I was watching and leave. So I would go and put the returns away, or shrink wrap the new display boxes, or dust the shelves. If that was all done I'd pop over to Brocks Used Books. Brock looked like if Santa Clause was a biker. He had a big white beard, always wore a red bandana on his head, and had a lazy right eye. He was also one of the kindest people

I had met to that point (and likely, since). He treated me like I mattered. We would talk about interesting stories, I'd tell him about my favorite movies, he'd tell me about a book that was similar. He was a friend. For Christmas the first year I knew him he gave me and all seven of my siblings a $25 credit in his store. He started saving Calvin and Hobbes, Garfield, and MAD Magazine books for me, and after I'd clearly gone well past the $25 he continued to give me books, always saying that he was *"sure there's still a little something on the account."* Then one day I showed interest in a different kind of book. Brock walked next door and asked my mom if she minded if I read it, and she said she didn't care. Since it was a newer book and in demand, Brock said I could just read it there. If anyone came in looking for a copy, and he didn't have any left on the shelf, he'd just sell them the copy I was reading. So I crawled under a sagging, A-frame bookshelf, laid down, and opened the first book that changed my life. It took me more than a year to read that book, and by the time I was done with it, Brock gifted me a copy (I'd gone through a few as people kept coming in looking for a copy). That book was the first time I ever felt seen. It was a safe training ground for the horrors that presented themselves in my real life. That book saved my life. That author saved my life. Then that author taught me how to tell a story. That book was IT.

This collection is dedicated to two people. Brock from Brock's Used Books, who I never got to say goodbye to. And to Stephen King, for showing me that the dark corners are only really scary if you're afraid to look into them, and for giving me teachers and friends in the Losers Club.

Coffee Table of Contents
(because they're short)

Scissors:
A Love Story

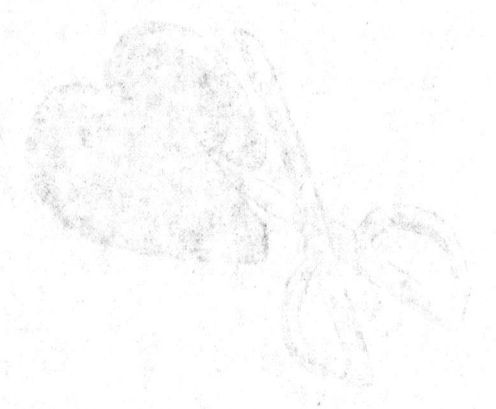

I was always happy to be a pair of scissors. I mean, I see the pencil and he gets worn down to a nub pretty quickly. Sure, he serves a great purpose—he gets to transcribe thought! That's pretty cool, but he doesn't last long. The pen has the same problem, unless you are one of those refillable jobs, but they are all arrogant pricks.

I'm a pair of scissors. I've got a great function: I cut, I create, I can help you make a snowflake out of a piece of paper or open that bag of food that will fuel human life, and that's value. One time I even cut Keith's hair when Erin promised him she could do a better job than the barber and they really didn't have the six bucks to spend for him to go anyway.

Now, I can't be blamed for the terrible job she did. I just set out about cutting the hair she wanted; I just did my job, as a good tool should.

This morning Keith used me to open a package that was delivered by some suit. Keith didn't look happy to be getting the delivery. I could see from the cup I normally sit in on the desk in the living room that he was furious. He scooped me up, opened me, and ran one of my blades under the fold in the top of the envelope, and I laid that sumbitch open like a champ! A razor couldn't have done a better job. The cut was clean and straight.

Keith dropped me onto the table rather than putting me back in the cup, which is okay, but sometimes they'll leave me there for days, and that can get boring. It's better in the cup. Plus, there's a new pink high-lighter I've been trying to get to know a little better.

I spent a good amount of time on the table today, watching Keith pace back and forth; at one point he got so mad that he punched a hole in the wall. His own wall! I can't fix that.

He said something about Erin and how he wasn't "giving her half of anything!" Erin hadn't been home in a few days, so I was beginning to wonder if she had finally left him like she'd been promising to do since last April when he left the computer on and his email open. She was yelling something about a "whore" when he got home that night. It wasn't pretty.

Keith's cell phone rang and he opened it. (Yet another device I wouldn't want to be: stuck in a pocket all day long, used a lot, and then just made obsolete and replaced like once a year! With a good sharpening I can last a lifetime.) Keith was yelling into the phone and telling someone, presumably Erin, that he refused to leave when she came by because he didn't want her to, quote, "steal his shit," which I took to mean the box of *Playboy* magazines and the pee-stained futon he brought when they moved in together.

When the call ended he flung the phone into the wall, where it exploded—yet another great reason not to be a cell phone.

An indeterminable amount of time passed before Erin walked through the front door. She was crying. Keith, still pacing the floor, finally came to an abrupt halt when he saw her.

"You have a lot of nerve having me served," Keith said.

He was a poet and didn't know it.

"I tried to talk to you about it, but you wouldn't stop yelling," Erin replied.

These arguments normally took place in the bedroom; it was harder to eavesdrop when they were in the room with the door closed, so I can't vouch for that.

"Just grab your clothes and get the fuck out of my house!" Keith said.

"*Your* house? I'm sorry, when was the last time you contributed a single cent for the rent?" Erin returned.

Cent for the rent. These two should have gone into writing lyrics for pop songs. Instead, Erin chose a career waiting tables and Keith took up the demanding hobby of trying to drink away his life and her money.

"I did more important things around this house than pay rent and you know that!" Keith said.

I assume he meant the time he tried to build a shelf in the living room. He ended up getting tired of working on it and just put a bunch of holes in the wall that were still very present in the décor.

"Just get out of my way so I can get my things and leave," Erin yelled.

She stormed past Keith and into the bedroom, slamming the door behind her. Keith was hot on her heels and the door bounced off his face, but not hard enough. It didn't latch. He opened it and went in with a huff.

I wondered if Erin would end up taking me with her. I know scissors aren't normally something one packs when separating stuff; we're more of a thing that often gets left in a drawer until someone moves and then just transported to the next place. I like to think Erin and I had a special relationship though.

I was adopted from a Kmart store during a Back-2-School sale for a buck, and I must say, it was a pretty good deal. I mean, she could have gone with one of those cheap jobs with the plastic handles, but she chose *me*, with my metal handle that made me feel sturdier in her hands. She was in the seventh grade at the time, so she took me to school that year, and when the school year ended she dropped me into the drawer of the pink and white desk in the corner of her bedroom. Oh, we would do everything together. We made crafts, I opened packages for her—I even cut the tags off of her first bra! That's friendship.

I was honored when she left for college and took only me and Stan. He's a ruler with both inches and centimeters—nothing too special, except he has a bit of cork on his back that helps him not slide around so much; he's a good dude and can still give you a straight line if you need one. At college, in her dorm room, I sat in an old soup can with some pens, pencils, and this cocky protractor who thought he knew *all* the angles.

Things were going well until she started sneaking Keith into the dorm room. Now, I'm not one to give out people's personals, but they did some messed-up stuff in that room. It wasn't long before Keith was there every single night, and then he started hanging out during the day too. I hated him. He once used me to groom himself—you know ... *down there*. I never recovered from that. Erin ended up getting tossed out of school when they found out she had a boy living with her; I think there was more to it than that, but it was hard to tell from the soup can.

So, I was thinking now, maybe she would see me on the table and take me with her? They were in the bedroom, screaming at each other—the door was open, but I could only make out a few words, and most of them were curses. Then there was a popping sound, and it went quiet for a split second before Erin started screaming. She ran out of the room with her hand on her red and swelling face.

"I can not believe you just hit me, you son of a bitch! I'm calling the police!"

She went for the phone on the wall of the kitchen. Before she could make it, though, Keith was on her; his arm shot out around her neck and he yanked her backward. She scratched at him, but his forearm just tightened around her neck. He dragged her back, bumping into the table I was sitting on. I slid a bit, my metallic side making that unmistakable sound as I crossed the wood surface.

I had to help her! I used all the willpower I had and tried to send her a message. And it must have worked, because she looked right at me.

She stretched out her hand and wrapped her soft fingers around me. It felt like heaven. She swung me upward. I felt the doughy flesh of Keith's right forearm give way to my points and I entered him right in the center of a (very douchey) Affliction tattoo. He screamed in pain and jerked his arm from me, pushing Erin away.

She fell forward onto the ground, and it was everything I could do to turn myself sideways so I didn't impale her as she landed on top of me, her soft breasts pressed against my side. For a moment I forgot all about the pink highlighter.

I was snapped back to reality when Erin quickly rolled onto her back and I saw the lumbering silhouette of Keith coming toward us. I wanted to yell at Erin to run, but I don't have a mouth or vocal cords, so instead I just tried to look as intimidating as possible.

Keith reached for Erin, and I pushed forward hard and found my mark in the center of his left hand. I punched through with ease, my metal shaft ripping through muscle and skin and popping out through the back side of his hand. He recoiled again, pulling me free.

I was dripping with blood by this point, but it felt . . . *good*. Normally a knife would get to pull this kind of duty, but right now it was my turn. I was the tool for this job, and my job wasn't finished.

With a scream, Erin lunged forward and buried me to the hilt below Keith's neck. I entered just under the collarbone, nicking it as I jumped in. I felt a twinge of pain as one of my tips caught the coarse bone and broke off. I dug deep and ripped at everything I could find before being yanked out again.

The cool air felt great after being in the hot mess that was Keith's chest. My relief was short-lived. I was plunged immediately back in, over and over again. I lost count of the number of strikes. It was just so *invigorating*. The pressure as I broke the skin and the suction of being pulled out. It was an almost sexual experience, Erin using me to do her most intimate business.

I dove deep into Keith's left side, managed to find a crease between two ribs, and slid directly into his lung. A burst of air shot out as I poked nearly an inch into the soft, life-giving tissue, and then I was out again.

I could see Keith's face, twisted and fighting to scream. He deserved this. He could have used the clippers in the drawer to trim the hair around his junk.

Erin thrust again. This time I struck him hard in the sternum; a cracking noise accompanied the brittle feel of punching through bone, and then I found my target in his heart.

Warm blood pulsed around me for a moment, before I felt the world shift.

I could feel Erin's hand loosen and then release me.

Everything shook before coming to a rest.

I could hear Erin's soft, muffled cries.

I sat, lodged in Keith's heart, for God knows how long. The blood had ceased flowing hours ago, and the sticky plasma was starting to harden around me, trapping me like a woolly mammoth in a tar pit.

Then I felt it: Erin's tender fingers slid through the holes in my handle and started to pull. It took a moment for me to free myself from the bone, but once I did it was only a matter of her pulling me out and I was back in the light of the apartment.

Erin sat on her knees next to Keith's lifeless body, just staring at me. I felt like the only office supply in the world. But I was more than that—I was a murder weapon now! Erin and I were accomplices! We were like Bonnie and Clyde! It was fantastic.

She wiped what blood she could from me and onto Keith's pants; she may have used his shirt, but it looked bloodier than me. After I was clean she set me on the table again, then set out to rolling him into a blanket and wrapping trash bags around him. She nabbed me again and I cut the thick strips of duct tape she used to secure the bags. It was nice. Not only did I help her kill him, but I was helping her hide the body. This was true teamwork.

She tucked me into her back pocket when she left, and my mind raced. I could feel the amazing curve of her butt as her jeans pulled me against her. When she got in the car, however, she wrapped me in a fast-food napkin and set me in the cupholder, where I flopped around a bit. We stopped, and I couldn't see what was happening, but she picked me up and carried me somewhere.

The next thing I knew she was holding me up to her face.

She kissed me, there in the sunset on a bridge overlooking the mighty Mississippi river.

Eternity flew by in that moment. I lost myself in the feel of her lips, and then, before I could protest, I was cast forward into the air.

I opened and cartwheeled through the air before splashing down into the cold water.

I sank into the darkness, the world closing around me as I settled in the murk and mud on the riverbed. I sit, like a confused crab, to this day on the bottom of that mighty river that one Samuel Clemens dedicated his life to, another lost relic in time.

But one that served a purpose.

Soft, Chewy Center

I van never really left the house. It wasn't that he was afraid to, it was just that the world as a whole fucking sucked, a lot. He hated most people, as they, themselves, fucking sucked a lot, too. It was nearly impossible to go anywhere without running into people that sucked. So he stayed in. He ran a website development company making microsites: little websites that were basically placeholders or redirection sites. People filled out a form on his website, put in what they wanted, and he made the site. He would have to email them when he was done, and sometimes they would want changes, but for the most part he had next to no interaction with the real world.

The only companionship he needed was that of his cat. The cat was all gray with a white patch on his face that looked like a beard, so Ivan named him Gandalf. Gandalf the Grey, specifically, but he just called him Gandalf unless he was upset with him—*then* he would use the full name.

Being able to get fast food delivered, and groceries, and really anything a person could want, was a game changer. It was so easy to be an introvert now. Ivan was living the dream.

"Gandalf, what shall we order for dinner?" Ivan asked, entering the outdated kitchen, in the outdated house, in the outdated neighborhood where he resided.

The cat did not answer, of course, other than to sit on the back of the couch and flop his tail a single time, signaling that he indeed did not give a single fuck. Though they both knew that if the food was not to his liking he would most certainly be "missing" the litter box that night.

"Maybe we order burgers? Or tacos?"

Gandalf did not respond. Not even a tail flop.

"Fine, I'll order from that Chinese place you like."

Ivan picked up his phone to place the on-line order.

"I'm getting crab rangoons, and you can't have any."

At this Gandalf lifted his head to scowl.

"Fine. You can have one."

Ivan filled the order with various combo plates and treats, knowing that he would have leftovers. Gandalf would be happy to eat any and all of it. If Ivan let him. Which he probably would, which is why the cat was a third the size of a balrog.

When Ivan was finished filling his cart he clicked the "contactless delivery" option, left a more-than-generous tip, as he always did, and submitted the order. The unspoken rule of food delivery was that if you tipped in advance, and the tip was large enough, your order would get priority and you would see it much, much sooner.

Sure enough, it took less than half an episode of *The Great British Bake Off* before the notification buzzed on his phone that someone was coming up the walk toward his front door. He watched in the app as the young woman set the food down, rang the doorbell, waited for a moment to see if there would be any response through the speaker (there wasn't, there never was), then took her leave. Once Ivan was satisfied that she was gone he opened the door, leaned out as far as he could without stepping out onto the porch, and snatched the handle of the cardboard box the food order was in.

When he set it on the table he noticed there were five fortune cookies, which was pretty standard. They always assumed that with the amount of food he ordered he must be feeding multiple people. They would be wrong. It was feeding just one person—and one exceptionally spoiled cat—for multiple days.

Ivan pulled out the containers, spreading them out like a buffet, cataloging them each as he went.

"Well, what's this?" he asked Gandalf as he pulled a plastic-wrapped tray from the box, holding it up to get a closer look.

There, under the cellophane, were five pale, pink treats. They had a translucent exterior, and resembled something halfway between a raw chicken wing and an éclair with no frosting. The restaurant never labeled the food, but Ivan had thought that if they were going to send something new, something extra, they would at least tell him what it was.

"Must be because I tipped so well. A little something extra," he said.

Ivan poked one with his finger. It was soft, like a gummy. He squeezed the package, putting his thumb on the one closest to the edge and pressing. There was some give, but it felt like there might be something inside.

"Feels like it's filled," he said. He looked down at the cat on the floor as if *he* could shed some light on the mysterious treats. "What do you think, Gandalf? Should I call and ask if this was meant for someone else?"

The cat gave no response other than to jump up onto the counter and sniff at the package.

"That's not for you," Ivan said, pulling the treats away and palming Gandalf in the face.

It wasn't immediately obvious what these mystery treats were for, but Ivan was always hoping to try new things. He hooked a finger into the plastic and pulled, ripping it open. He lifted it to his nose and took a deep sniff. The smell was sharp and familiar. Was it cumin? No, too sharp for that. Coriander, maybe. Something with some musk to it.

The limp, sticky treat was soft between his fingers as he peeled it off the styrofoam tray. He squeezed it. The outside was pliable, squishy, and a touch rubbery. There was a rigidity to it, though. He grasped each end between his thumbs and forefingers and tore off a piece. Something popped, and warm liquid spilled out onto his palm.

"Pretzel," he told Gandalf. "And jam, maybe?"

The cat just stuck out his nose, inviting Ivan to let him sample it for himself.

"You only live once, right? Anthony Bourdain would be so proud."

Ivan popped the small bit into his mouth and chewed.

"Ah—it's raw," he said, spitting the masticated bit into the trash. "Wasn't bad, but I think it might be chicken. You can't eat raw chicken. You could get sick. These people are trying to kill me by not labeling these things."

Ivan plopped the leftover piece of the treat onto a plate, covered it with a paper towel, and set it in the microwave, punching the button for raw poultry.

He looked down into the disapproving face of his cat.

"What? It's just that one. If it's good, I'll try a few methods. Maybe baked, or fried. Oh, we can try one in the air fryer. I bet that would be good."

The cat didn't seem to care. He would gladly take a treat any way that Ivan would give it to him.

A pop startled Ivan and he turned to see a pink mist settling in the microwave. He punched the button, and the door swung open. Bits of gore clung to the inside. He covered his nose against the rancid smell.

"I think it's bacon-wrapped, bone-in chicken. Or maybe some other kind of bird? What other bird do we eat the wings of?"

Gandalf didn't answer. He was busy nosing at the package on the counter.

Ivan brushed him away with the back of his hand.

Billy Ray Carver sat in the exam room, the paper gown he'd been given clinging to his sweaty skin. It wasn't the first time he'd been paid to participate in a medical trial, but it was the sketchiest. He'd never had to enter a clinic through a Chinese restaurant before. He didn't like the idea that they may be storing things from both places in the same refrigerator. He overlooked his unease because the ad had promised $13,000 for less than three days' worth of testing. After he'd passed the initial tests for the study, the doctor had told him that, if the medicine worked, he would be asleep for most of the study, so he was to notify anyone who may be worried about him that he would be unreachable for the next few days. That was easy enough, he'd told them. He had no family. Outside of driving a ride-share, he didn't have a job. He hadn't had a girlfriend in about three years. So he was the perfect candidate.

"Mr. Carver, you're all set," the nurse, or whoever it was who had been jamming him with needles for the last hour, said.

"So now what?" Billy replied. "Do I get to do the study?"

"Yes, sir. You are a qualified candidate for the study."

"Since I'm an ideal candidate, can you finally tell me what it is we're doing?"

"A *qualified* candidate," she corrected. "I cannot share any of the information of the study, but I do need to have you sign these papers before the next phase."

The nurse offered a thick packet of paper that was too big for a paperclip, so instead it was secured with a large binder clip in the corner.

"What exactly am I signing?"

"Standard indemnification forms. This releases us from liability if there are unforeseen consequences of the trial."

"That doesn't seem right," Billy said. "I'm not an expert, but I'm pretty sure you can't just test things on people and not have any accountability."

"Would you like to forfeit your position in the trial?" the woman said, taking the packet of paper from Billy.

"No, no, I didn't say that. I just want to know what we're doing, that's all."

"A deep sleep study," came a voice from the door, which Billy did not hear open. It was a man who appeared to be in his mid-thirties. He was good-looking, but almost too good-looking. The kind of good-looking that made you immediately suspicious of a person.

"Are you the guy running this thing? The one who can provide some sort of details as to what the hell we'll be doing?"

"I am Dr. Riddick, and yes, this is my study," the man said, taking the stack of papers from the nurse and passing them back to Billy. "This is a highly incentivized trial, Mr. Carver. If you choose not to participate, there will be no hard feelings. We have a long list of candidates who are excited for the opportunity."

"I just want to know what the opportunity entails," Billy said.

"That's understandable. But until the nondisclosure agreements are signed, we are unable to share information about the trial. You understand, right?"

"I mean, I guess so. It just makes it hard to agree to anything if I don't know what I'm agreeing to, ya know?"

"I do, of course," the doctor said. "What I can tell you is that we are working on a long-term, sustainable, deep sleep study. Think of something akin to hibernation."

"Like what bears do?" Billy asked.

"Similar, yes. Very good. Though ours is much more controlled. A bear doesn't sleep straight through winter the way we think of it. They are restless and wake often to check and see what's out there. We take a more methodical approach. But I really can't say any more without the paper being signed."

"Thirteen grand?" Billy asked, confirming the payment that was offered in the ad.

"Ah . . . that's actually a bit of a misrepresentation of the compensation for this study."

"Of course it is. The old bait and switch."

Billy tried to hand the papers back to the doctor, who refused them.

"No, what I mean is, that is just the beginning of the compensation structure. The initial payment, if you will."

"Huh?" was all Billy could manage.

"The thirteen thousand dollars is for the first test. If you are found to be a good recipient of the . . ." The doctor paused. He appeared to consider his next words before continuing. ". . . the product, then you will be offered the opportunity to participate in the next stage. Which pays considerably more."

"How considerably?" Billy asked.

"Ten times more," the doctor said, placing a pen into a hand Billy didn't know he was raising.

"Is it dangerous?" Billy asked, signing the papers next to all the *X*s.

Dr. Riddick took the packet, flipped through to be sure everything was signed, and nodded his approval before continuing.

"It isn't *not* dangerous. But we are far enough along in the process to where adverse effects have been majorly limited."

"So now I've signed, tell me what we are doing," Billy insisted.

"Have you heard of hypersleep, Mr. Carver?"

"Like in the movies?"

"Yes, like in the movies. When they have to send someone on a mission, say to Mars, or a different galaxy, and they put them to sleep in a cryogenic chamber."

"Is that what we're doing? Cryosleep?"

"No. Our technology is more organic. I can explain it, if you'd like. But it tends to be unpleasant," the doctor said.

"Tell me," Billy replied.

"We, for lack of a better way of explaining, feed you a parasite. This parasite will then begin putting your body into a state of paralysis that will allow you to go into a hypersleep that will cause your body to stay in a stasis that could last indefinitely."

"I'm sorry . . . so you're telling me you're going to feed me some weird bug that will put me in a coma?"

"Sort of, yes. It's painless, so you don't have to worry about that," the doctor said.

"And what happens to my body? Won't I die of dehydration or something?"

"No, of course not. The parasite is unique in that once it attaches to the host it uses the host's body to begin production of the very nutrients that host requires to survive. We have a rat, a species with an expected lifespan of about three years, who has been alive for nearly ten years in this state. All vitals are good, brain function is solid, and if we woke her up tomorrow she would be as healthy as the day we fed her the product."

"How big is the thing I have to eat?" Billy asked. He'd seen people eat some pretty disgusting things on TV game shows, and it was always the part he didn't think he could handle.

"Well, unfortunately, the parasites are not effective on a full-sized adult. It would take multiple to get you into that state, and they are very, very expensive."

Billy thought about it and found it unnerving. He didn't want to eat any bugs, but it was too late to say no, and for the amount of money they were offering he didn't want to rock any boats either.

Ivan was not dismayed or deterred after the failure of the first treat. He set a small pot with oil to heat as he cleaned out the microwave. Wiping away what could have been a delicacy but instead was a pink slime with small chunks in it. This would be tossed into the trash, leaving just four more chances to get the treats right. Yes, he could call the restaurant and ask how they should be prepared, but then he would have to talk to someone, and fuck that.

Crackling oil puckered the outer layer of the next treat as Ivan lowered it into the oil. It began browning almost immediately.

"These better not make me sick," he said, turning the treat in the pan to cook it evenly.

Once it was nice and crispy, he removed it from the oil and placed it on a plate lined with a paper towel. Then, when the external temperature wasn't that of the surface of the sun, Ivan took a bite. This one was better—or at least the crust was. The inside hadn't cooked properly and had the texture and taste of uncooked meat.

"I think it's pasta. Like manicotti, maybe? But it ain't bad."

Ivan pulled a piece of the crust off and gave it to Gandalf, who seemed more than happy to gobble it up.

Perhaps a parboil was the way to go. Cook the inside with the boil and then the outside with oil. That should be perfect. He tore off another piece of the crust for Gandalf, and chucked the treat into the garbage before setting a pot of water to boil.

"So I would just lay there?" Billy asked the doctor.

"Not necessarily. The parasite also causes a secretion that forms an outer layer. Like a cocoon of sorts."

"Gross. I don't want to be in a cocoon. Is it slimy?"

"You will never be aware of the cocoon. You ingest the parasite and then you fall asleep. The parasite will then induce the simulated coma. Once you are in a stable state the outer dermal layer will begin to blossom, similar to that of a chrysalis of a butterfly."

Billy sat back, sucking in a chestful of air, attempting to help buy himself time to think.

"Then what?"

"That's where things get tricky."

Which is not what you want a doctor to say, Billy thought.

"More tricky than turning into a fuckin' human centipede?"

"Butterfly," the doctor corrected.

"I don't know, man. This sounds fucked-up. I don't want to eat a parasite."

"You have signed the contract already," the doctor reminded him.

"Shit . . . What does the parasite look like? How big is it?"

A five-minute boil, followed by the oil, didn't seem to help the flavor. The inside of the treat was soft and chewy and the outside was crisp, but something was off. There were crunchy bits that didn't seem properly prepared. He added a bit of salt and a touch of hot sauce, and he was closer to where he wanted to be, but not there yet. He finished the whole thing, only leaving the tiniest piece for Gandalf. Only two treats left, though, and he wanted to see if he could really figure out the best way to get the most out of it.

"I'd rather not focus on the size of the parasite, but it is smaller than you think, I'm sure," the doctor explained. "There are more difficult things to focus on in the trial, so it is best to just trust that we have put a lot of effort into doing this all the correct way."

"What sort of difficult things are we talking about?" Billy asked.

"We don't really discuss the full unpleasantries of the procedure with patients. The science of it is new, and it really isn't something that can be explained without multiple doctorates in various fields."

"Try me," Billy challenged.

"The parasite is a microorganism that must be ingested. It secretes a mitochondrial fluid that forces your body into a sleeplike state."

"That's it?"

"Well, no. Again, I really think you would be better off not knowing the fine details, as, like I have mentioned, it is unpleasant to see, but you shouldn't experience any of it. Think of it like surgery."

"Except I have to eat a bug first."

"A parasite. A relatively small one," the doctor said.

Ivan started with a sous vide for a few hours to bring the meat up to the perfect temp before moving it to preheated oil for a light fry. He only did one, not wanting to spoil the rest of the meal, but if it worked he'd make the other and have it for a late-night snack.

Ivan pushed the treat around on his plate. His best laid plans had not panned out the way he had thought, unfortunately. The inside still had too much crunch and a slightly bitter, iron taste. The sous vide hadn't done enough to soften it. The first bite was the worst. The snap of what could only be bone made him gag. He reached in and pulled the hard bit from his mouth. It was bone, but it was more dense than any chicken wing he had seen.

"What the fuck did they feed me?" Ivan said, trying not too hard to think about whatever it might be. He pushed the half-eaten treat into the garbage and tossed the plate into the dishwasher.

He pulled the package containing the last treat from the refrigerator and picked at it, attempting to investigate whatever mystery meat lay beneath, but just looking at the raw meat made him feel sick. He dropped it on the counter with the intent of trying to search out photos of it and see if he could solve the mystery.

"Come on, Gandalf." He scooped the cat up under the belly and hauled him away from the treat he so badly wanted to get.

Billy sat with the other candidates for the trial, each seeming just as desperate and confused as him. They were told not to speak to one another, but then they were left in a room alone. There was no way they weren't going to discuss what they knew, and more importantly, what they didn't.

"They tell you guys about the parasite?" one of the others asked. He appeared to be in his mid-thirties and had the distinct sunken cheeks and scabbed forehead of someone struggling with addiction. Billy had never had that particular demon, but he knew it well enough and felt an immediate sense of empathy for the guy.

"What parasite?" a lady asked. She was younger, maybe early twenties. She didn't look like she was in the throes of addiction, but she'd maybe seen some hard times.

"They said we gotta eat some fucking bug or something," another man said. He was about Billy's age, heavier, probably a few inches taller.

"It's not a bug," Billy said. "It's a parasite."

"What the fuck do you think a parasite *is*?" the larger man barked.

"It could be a microscopic organism, dingus," Billy retorted. "I saw you in the locker room when we were changing. I suspect microscopic organisms are something you know a bit about."

"I'm gonna kill you," the man snapped, standing and taking a step toward Billy.

"Sit down and shut up, both of you," an older woman said from the far bed in the room. She'd been the most distant, hadn't made eye contact with anyone until that point. "If you ruin this for me and I don't get paid, I'll kill you both."

The door opened and a young man stepped in. His soft shoes made almost no sound on the tile floor. He wore the same nurse's scrubs as the woman who had done the tests.

"You here to shed some light on all of this?" Billy asked.

"I'm here to get you out of here," the man said.

"What if we don't *want* to get out of here?" the woman in the corner asked.

"Why should we leave?" Billy asked, in a slightly more understanding tone.

"The rat," the man in the scrubs said.

"What rat?" the large, angry man asked, still standing. "I ain't eating no rat."

Billy answered. "The one he said has been asleep for like nine years?"

"That's the one. There are things they didn't tell you. Bad things," the man in the scrubs said.

"What sort of bad things?" Billy asked.

A door down the hall opened and footsteps echoed.

"The rat has maintained brain activity. It's been awake the entire time," the man said, looking over his shoulder to make sure that the doctor hadn't entered the room yet.

"That's it?" the big man asked. "It's only for three days. I can handle that for this kind of money."

"After the first trial, depending on how bad it is, we can decide if it's worth it to do it for longer and a lot more money," Billy said.

"But you are awake, in a paralyzed state. You see, hear, and feel *everything*," the man pleaded. "It's cruel."

"But you're in a warm little cocoon. It's like a protective shell," Billy argued, holding his hands up to his chest to simulate snuggling into a sleeping bag.

"You haven't seen the rat," the man counters. "It's hideous. You don't want to see an animal like that."

The unmistakable sound of glass shattering woke Ivan from his nap in the oversized chair in front of his television.

Gandalf was no longer nestled between his feet on the raised footrest of the chair.

"Gandalf?" he called into the kitchen.

The sound that came back in response was that of the cat knocking something over on the counter.

"Gandalf?" he called again, sitting up and tucking the footrest back in before pulling himself out of the chair.

The kitchen was a mess. Flour coated the counter, dotted with paw prints going from one end all the way to the other. Broken glass lay scattered around the floor, small shards twinkling in the fluorescent light. The package for the treats lay empty, the last treat seemingly scratched free by a hungry tabby.

"Gandalf!" Ivan shouted when he saw the cat on the far corner of the counter, behind the microwave.

The door opened and the doctor came in pushing a metal cart with a number of syringes, some gauze, and a styrofoam tray.

"Jacobs, are the subjects ready?" the doctor asked, pulling one of the syringes up and studying its contents closely.

The man in the scrubs turned and looked the group over once more. His face pleaded with them to change their minds.

"We're ready," the lady in the corner said before Jacobs could answer.

The doctor looked around the room, and the others, including Billy, nodded in agreement.

"Excellent," the doctor said. "Everyone take your places on your beds, please. Jacobs, get the door."

"Gandalf, leave it!" Ivan yelled, pushing the cat off the counter and away from the chewed-up treat. It was messy, bloody, and it looked like Gandalf had taken more than a few bites of it after dragging it to the corner. The cat landed on the floor and ran away, leaving small drops of blood and footprints of flour as he went.

There was a part of the test the subjects hadn't been made aware of. A part that was vitally important for the microorganisms to do their part. The doctor had told them that the parasites were too small for a full-grown human. What he hadn't told them was that they wouldn't be full-grown humans when they were given the parasites. The largest creature they'd gotten it to work on was the rat, and they were lucky with that. So they had another plan.

The first shots the subjects got were to dope them up so they wouldn't resist the second. Once they were as high as Snoop Dogg at a Willie Nelson concert in Denver, they were administered a drug that caused their cells to contract. The doctor explained it all while it was happening, but Billy could only remember so much thanks to the drugs. What was very clear in his memory, though, was the pain of his muscles tightening as his legs began to pull across the bed, then up through the paper gown he wore. He felt his hands slide, limp and lifeless, across the mattress he lay on. There was a great pressure in his eyes as they shrank in his skull before his skull caught up. The last part to shrink was his tongue; it had felt like it was growing in his mouth, not that his mouth was shrinking around his tongue, but either way, he was worried that he was going to choke on it. His body shriveled and compacted in on itself, leaving him no bigger than the action figures he played with as a child.

At first he was convinced that it was all part of a bad trip from the drugs he'd been given, but then the doctor lifted his entire body inside one hand and placed him on the styrofoam tray. Once Billy was there, the doctor used a dropper to place liquid in his mouth, explaining that it would take very little time for the parasite to work.

He was correct. Within minutes Billy felt it squirming around inside of him. First in his stomach, and then his intestines. At one point he was sure it was trying to escape through his anus, so he tried to pucker it up, but his body was no longer his to control.

He could hear, see, and feel everything, but everything else belonged to the parasite now.

Billy felt the gel begin to form on his lips. It felt like layer upon layer of balm had been applied and not wiped away. The feeling spread, first down his chest and abdomen, then his crotch and legs felt the thick covering as well. Then it moved over his face, covering his nose and eyes. That was the moment the claustrophobia set in. He could no longer take in breath, he was fully cocooned, but had he been breathing before that? He wasn't sure.

The parasite had done its job.

It wasn't long before he passed out, but he didn't stay asleep for long.

Billy felt woozy, but he managed to get his eyes opened fully, though it was hard to see through the thick jell that had congealed over his face. It wasn't just his face, but his whole body. Panic set in. He couldn't move. He was paralyzed. The cocoon surrounding him felt sticky and rubbery against his skin, but he couldn't adjust. He was stuck.

The terrifying event would have still been worth the thirteen thousand dollars, had it gone the way it was supposed to. Jacobs, however, had other plans. As soon as the group was fully encased in the goop, lined up like little Hot Pockets on the tray, and cellophane was wrapped around them for storage, they were placed in a small refrigerator where they would be left for the three days of the trial. That was when Jacobs returned, pulling them from the fridge, waking them up, and telling them he was going to get them out of there.

The doctor gave chase and Jacobs fled through the front of the Chinese restaurant, ditching the tray in a box awaiting delivery.

Billy was unsure of Jacobs's fate, but he was very aware of his own: the five helpless subjects were now being delivered to a hungry customer, along with what felt like enough orange chicken for a small army.

Billy passed out at some point during the delivery but woke again when the tray was pulled from the box and dropped. There was a man there who he didn't recognize. The terror of seeing a giant was still new to him, and he remembered the story of "Jack and the Beanstalk," where the giant walked around shouting "Fee-fi-fo-fum!" and trying to kill Jack. That became his reality as he watched one person after another pulled from the tray by the giant and murdered in horrific ways. He knew they could all feel it. He watched the calm young woman's feet get ripped off before being blown up in the microwave. Then watched the angry, large man get deep-fried. (That one he didn't mind as much.) Then one was boiled, which hopefully killed him before he was fried. Then the woman from the corner, who was cooked very, very slowly, and then fried. If he understood the sous vide process more, he may have felt even worse about her fate, but he chose to believe she died quickly and painlessly.

After tossing the last of the other subjects into the garbage, the giant took his cat and left, leaving Billy alone to await his fate.

An hour passed, then two, before the sounds of tiny little feet pitter-patting across the floor drew Billy's attention. His field of vision was filled with the face of the cat, who nosed at the cocoon curiously.

Billy wanted to yell. He wanted to scream and scare the cat off, but he still had no control over his body.

The cat's claws poked into the soft surface of the cocoon, tearing carefully, trying to inspect what was in there. Billy's body rocked with the motion. Sharp teeth poked through, coming dangerously close to Billy's face as the cat pulled off a small piece of the outer layer. It seemed to decide that it did not like the taste of that, that it wanted what was inside instead. Searing pain stabbed through Billy's cheek as the cat dug its claw into the hole it had created with its teeth, attempting to free the treat within.

Billy felt something in his gut. The parasite. It moved. First scurrying up into his stomach under his chest cavity, and then back down to his sphincter, pushing itself out with equal parts relief and pain. As soon as it was out, Billy felt something else. His pinky moved. He wiggled it against the tight confines of the cocoon.

The cat dug in again, its claw ripping Billy's cheek from his face. The point of the claw clanked across his teeth like a xylophone. He tried to scream, but he didn't have that much control yet.

His chest bucked and his lungs began to move again, drawing breath through the mutilated side of his face. It wasn't obvious if it was the gore or the fact that its prey was living that drove the cat into a frenzy, but it began tearing full force at the cocoon. Teeth and claws dug into it, puncturing through and ripping flesh from Billy's body in ribbons.

Billy screamed. Blood filled his throat. He coughed to clear it, but as it stood then, he was drowning in his own blood. He tried to tense every muscle to regain use of his body. Slowly, one by one, his limbs responded. He just hoped it wouldn't be too late, as the cat was almost through the only armor he had to protect him from being devoured.

A sharp pain ripped across his abdomen as a claw laid him open. The gel in front of him parted as he forced himself to sit up. Blood pooled in the sack he had been laying in, making it slick, so that getting to his feet was even more difficult in his weak state, but he tried. He rolled to one side, clutching his gut and pushing up from his knees. Pain shot through his body as the cat sank its teeth into both sides of the back of Billy's neck, wrenching him upward from the cocoon. Blood ran down his legs and dripped onto the counter as the cat ferried him across, not giving any care to the water glass on the counter or the measuring cup full of flour that it knocked over in an attempt to get its prize to a place it could enjoy it, away from the prying eyes of anyone who would attempt to take it away.

The beast carried him across the counter, hunkering down behind the microwave that, to Billy, was bigger than a two-story house. The acceptance of death washed over Billy as the cat held tight to his neck. The pain from the teeth rubbing against the nerves there actually made him *hope* for death. A quick one, preferably.

Then he saw it. Something from the corner of his eye. The giant had woken and was ambling toward them. If he hurried, he could get there in time.

Billy tried to scream, but his throat had suffered so much damage that what came out was merely a weak, inaudible, gurgling moan.

"Gandalf!" the giant cried.

What the fuck? Billy thought. What an oddly timed pop-culture reference.

"Gandalf!" Ivan yelled, swatting the cat away. It dropped the messy treat onto the counter and scurried away. "Oh, my god."

Ivan leaned down and looked at the bloody mess.

"I've got to get something, hold on," he said, leaving the mass of flesh and bone dripping on the counter while he raced across the kitchen. He returned with a paper towel. He gently scooped up what was left of the treat and carried it over to the sink, where he turned on the water and began carefully rinsing the misshapen mass in the paper towel.

Gandalf meowed up at him. Ivan looked down at the cat, whose maw was speckled with blood.

"No, you can't have it!" he said, looking back at the thing in his hand. "I don't even know what the fuck it is."

He dropped the thing from the paper towel into the sink. It bounced off the side of the drain before disappearing through the rubber flaps above the disposal. The flip of a switch brought a grinding sound of flesh and bone being rendered to paste. Ivan turned up the water and washed the blood down the drain until the sound of the motor and teeth was smooth once again.

"Next time," he said to the cat, "we're having burgers."

IN THE DARK WE SIN

When I was seventeen I got drunk for the first time. My neighbor and I swiped a thirty-pack of Keystone Lights out of a stack of cases my father was saving in the garage for the Fourth of July. That stack of alcohol stretched from the floor to the ceiling, so we never thought anyone would notice if we pilfered just one case. Our little crime of the century may have gone unnoticed if I hadn't stumbled into the house later that night, completely bombed out of my gourd, and ran into my father as he was sneaking down the stairs for a late-night snack and a cigarette. He knew immediately that I was hammered, and I was too drunk to lie when he asked where I got the suds. I don't remember what happened after that. I don't know if the lack of memory is because I was drunk or because my father smashed a thick glass ashtray against the side of my head and knocked me the fuck out, but either way I had no idea what had happened when I woke up the next morning in a concoction of blood, urine, vomit, and sweat, all of which I hope were my own, on the tile floor of our entryway.

Over the twenty years since then, I've been knocked out plenty of times. A few from being punched in bar fights and brawls in jail. Twice I was choked out, once by an angry cellmate, once by a happy girlfriend. What I am trying to tell you is that losing consciousness is not new to me. It's old hat at this point. So when I feel cold steel beneath my face, I don't even have to open my eyes to know that I got laid out. Last thing I remember I left the halfway house with my papers in my hand. I was heading uptown to see if I could find an apartment to rent. I must have stepped in front of a car, or looked at someone the wrong way, because here I am, once again, waking up somewhere I don't remember being.

My eyelids feel heavy and they fight me to open. I hear a water droplet splash somewhere nearby, and the echo it makes reminds me of my days hanging out in the lower levels of the prison on less-than-desirable details. I can hear a few other people, some light murmur of voices and sounds of confusion. I start to wonder if I was involved in something bigger. Maybe like a 9/11–type thing. I force my eyes open, but for a moment I wonder if they opened at all. It is pitch-black. Not dark. Pitch-black. The complete absence of light.

"Ay, what happened?" I say out into the darkness.

Something brushes against me and I push myself up onto my hands and knees.

"What was that?"

"Yo, take it easy," a voice says in the dark.

"Hello?" another voice says.

"Who's there?" Another voice.

"Am I blind or is it just real fucking dark in here?" I say, waving my hands back and forth trying to get an idea of my surroundings.

"If you are, we all are," a deeper, more confident voice echoes loudly.

"Where are we?" I ask.

"Your guess is as good as any," the deep voice says, booming through the room. I can feel it in my bones when he talks.

"Sounds like underground somewhere," one of the voices says. As if to confirm this, there's another echoing drip.

"Anyone got a cell phone they can turn on and get some light?" I ask.

"Mine's gone," a voice says.

"Mine too!" a more nervous voice replies.

"Mine too, and my flashlight," the deep voice says. "Everything but my clothes is gone."

"Were we in an accident?" I ask.

"Who knows? I just woke up down here a minute ago," a voice says.

A variety of different voices reply:

"Me too."

"Same."

"Yep. Me too."

"Me as well."

"Yeah."

"I think I was the first to wake up," a voice says that sounds slightly farther away. I turn my head to listen closely to where it is coming from.

"What's happening?" a whiny, groggy voice says. It sounds like it's down and to my right. I hear whoever it is scrambling.

"Quiet!" the deep voice says.

"What is going on?" the groggy voice begs. "I can't see anything! Why can't I see anything?"

I hear a heavy footstep fall to my right, then another, moving toward me.

"Shut up!" the deep voice demands. "Who said they were the first to wake up?"

"What is going on?" the whiny voice asks again.

"I said shut up," the deep voice says.

Another few steps toward me and something moves through the air past my shoulder.

"Hey!" I shout. My instincts tell me it was a kick.

There are a few more steps, then another kick that doesn't land.

"Everyone needs to shut the fuck up," the deep voice demands.

There is another drip. This one sounds bigger.

"What is happening here?" I say. I feel confident another kick will not come in my direction, now that everyone is quiet, but I put my hands up in the direction that the last few kicks came from just in case.

"Who said they were the first awake?" the deep voice says again. His voice echoes off multiple surfaces, which tells me he is turning his head and talking to everyone, but I don't think he can see since he missed with his kicks. He said he couldn't see, but I am not one to trust someone's word. Their actions are what I will base my opinion of them on every time.

"I think I was," the distant voice says.

I can hear the deep-voice man turn. "How long?" His voice is stern. He gives off a strong sense of confidence and control. My guess is he is an authority. Military, maybe? NYPD?

"I don't know. Maybe five minutes before the next person?" the voice says. It doesn't sound like it's getting any closer.

There is another drip, equally as big as the last, but the duration between this one and the last is shorter than the previous gap.

"Who was next?" the deep voice asks.

A few people speak at the same time, but none of them seem confident in what they are saying.

"Could have been me."

"Or maybe me. I just laid here for a minute."

"I have no idea."

Another drip.

"You, first awake, what is your name?" the deep voice says. I'm leaning toward police for his vocation. The military don't have to focus on calming folks down the way police do. He seems to be trying to get this guy on board.

Another drip, this one bigger. It hits the small puddle the others have made, and it must be closer than I thought because I feel a few drops of ice-cold water hit my leg.

"Ben. Ben Walker," the voice returns.

"Ben, I'm Dean. Officer Dean Kurds. I'd shake your hand, but I can't find it," the deep voice belonging to the man identifying himself as Officer Dean Kurds says. "Now, Ben, you are our greatest resource at the moment. You've been awake the longest, you are the farthest away, so you've explored a little. It seems like all of us were just piled up here in the middle and you are over there. Am I right?"

"When I woke up all I could hear was breathing from all of you. I was underneath one of you and my leg was stuck," Ben says.

"Yeah, when I came to I was underneath someone and they were climbing off of me," another voice says from behind me.

I can hear Dean turn. He is standing next to me. I am pretty sure I could reach out and touch his leg, but I really don't want to. There were five drips in his question-and-answer session.

"Sorry about that. I think that was me," another voice says from behind me.

"Okay, okay now. Let's take this one step at a time," Dean says, talking toward the voices behind me. "Ben, what did you do when you got off the pile?"

"I crawled on my hands and knees until I found a wall," Ben says.

"What kind of wall is it?" I ask without thinking. I stand up, feeling that if something is going to happen now I think I want to be standing for it. Plus, the knees of my jeans are starting to get wet from the spreading puddle made from the increasing drips.

"Huh?" Dean says. He seems to have noticed that not only am I now standing right next to him but that I have interrupted his line of questioning.

"It feels like metal. Just like the floor," Ben answers.

"Any doors?" Dean asks quickly.

"Not that I feel, but I haven't checked much of it," Ben says.

"Are we in a metal box?" Dean asks no one.

"I don't think so," I say.

I hear Dean turn quickly toward me. "No?"

I can feel the heat from his breath. I take a small step backward.

"And how exactly can you be sure of that?" he says.

"The echo," I say.

"The echo?"

"Yeah. If you talk toward Ben," I say, turning my body in that direction, "you get a hard echo that reverberates. If you turn this way—" I do a quarter turn. "Hello," I say. "And this way—" Another quarter turn. "Hello," I say, and pause so everyone can hear the echo.

"So?" Dean says.

"Turn around and talk."

I can hear him move. "Hello?" His voice is loud and rings off every surface it can find. "I don't hear a difference."

"Allow me, Darth Vader," I say, and turn in that direction. "Hello?" I say at the same volume I had before. The echo is present, but it is noticeably lower. Three drips happen in quick succession. The timing is no longer steady, and I assume that soon they will be a stream.

"Whoa," one of the voices behind me says.

"So where is that wall?" Dean says, and I can hear him shuffling carefully forward.

"It's there, but I don't think it is steel like the others," I say. I start shuffling forward but only make it a few steps before my foot hits something. It is soft and I know immediately that I have kicked someone. "I'm sorry," I say, but there is no response. I crouch and tap the body. It doesn't move, but I can feel it breathing. "Everyone be careful. We don't know how many more are still down," I say into the dark. I start to gently shake the person and I feel something beneath them that is different. They are lying in the water that has been dripping. I put my hand in the water, and I can feel it moving ever so slightly. I trace the line of water and can tell that it has run in the direction of the person lying in front of me. As I follow the water across the steel floor my finger drops suddenly. "Ope, I've got something here."

"What is it?" Dean demands as he turns toward me.

"I think it's a grate of some sort."

"Is it open?" He has shuffled up next to me, and I feel him kick the person in front of me. "That you?"

"No. There's a person unconscious on top of the grate," I say.

"Well, move them," Dean says. He reaches down and grabs at the body, pulling it with ease away from the grate. I feel the water start to move faster now that the block has been cleared. Within a second it hits the lip of the grate and begins to pour in.

I pull on the grate, but it doesn't budge.

"It feels like it's cut into the floor. It ain't opening. But it isn't very deep. I can hear the water hitting the bottom." I stick my finger in and can just barely feel the water pooling there.

"We must be in some sort of sewer holding tank or something," one of the other voices says.

"Well, let's find the damn door," Dean says as he starts shuffling toward the wall that didn't echo as much.

"Everyone wait a second." I stand and take a deep breath. "Everyone slowly make your way to the closest wall you can find, but be careful not to trip over anyone who may still be out. Crawl if you have to."

"Everyone stay where you are," Dean says into the void. "What good is that going to do anyone? We don't know what condition this space is in. If we were in a collapse or something, there could be hazards."

"I don't think we were involved in a hazard, Officer Kurds," I say, trying to give him enough respect that he doesn't see this as a power play.

"And how do you know that?" he asks.

"Just an educated guess."

"Yeah? And what education is that?"

I turn away from where Dean is so he doesn't think I am talking directly at him. "Can everyone who is awake, and can hear me, please count off? I'll start. One."

"Two," one of the voices behind me says.

"Three," another says.

"Four," another man in the dark that I don't recall hearing before says.

"Five," the whiny man says.

"Six," Ben says.

There is a pause. It is quiet minus the steady drip.

"Seven," Dean finally says.

Another pregnant pause.

"And our friend on the floor makes eight," I say.

"There is someone else over here who is still unconscious," Ben says.

"Okay, so nine?" I ask.

"I think so," Ben says.

"Your point?" Dean asks.

"Unless I am mistaken, and please forgive me if I am, but I didn't hear a single woman's voice. And the person I felt on the ground felt like he had a beard. So unless my Aunt Millie is down here, there's a solid chance it was a man too," I say. "Ben, without fondling anyone, can you tell if the sleeper you've got is a man or a woman?"

"Um," Ben starts. We listen as he moves around. "Some light stubble on the face. Feels like a dude."

"Anyone remember being knocked out?" I ask. "Because I don't."

"Not me," a voice says.

"Me neither."

"Nope."

"I was at the bank on Broadway and Grand," Ben says. "I had just walked out onto the sidewalk. I don't remember anything after that."

"I don't remember anything," someone else says.

"Ben," I say. "Manhattan, right?"

"Yeah," he replies.

"I was in Fordham Heights," I say. "Where were you, Dean?"

"Officer Kurds," Dean says.

"Sorry. Officer Kurds."

"I was just coming off a call in Marine Park."

"Am I right to assume everyone else was not anywhere near those three locations?" I ask.

"Not me," one voice says.

There is a pause, and in it I can hear that the water is now a solid trickle.

"I was in Flatbush," a voice says. "That isn't too far from Marine Park."

"Okay, that's fine, but Ben," I say, "that intersection you were in is always busy, right?"

"Yeah, it's always a pain."

"Right, so the last thing we all remember was being in fairly public places surrounded by other people, correct?"

I get a smattering of agreement, but no one says otherwise.

"Again, the point?" Dean says.

"If it was some random accident, how did we all get here from separate places? And if it was something random, how come there are only men in here with us?" I say and just let it sit.

It is silent minus the now running water. The hollow sound of it pouring into the grate has stopped. I don't want to point it out because I don't want to panic anyone, but I know that it means that the grate doesn't drain the water. If the pace at which the water speeds up continues, it will be pouring in here fairly soon.

"And how does everyone moving to the walls help us?" Dean asks.

"Well, once we get there I will show you," I say. "So, everyone carefully turn in a circle and say something to see if you can tell which wall you are closest to, then move toward it."

"Like echolocation," the whiny man says.

"Exactly, um—" I pause. "I'm sorry, what was your name, my friend?"

"Gary. I'm Gary."

"Great, Gary, I'm Crispin. And we've got Ben by the wall. How about everyone says their name to try and locate the closest wall? We get to know who is in here and we get where we're going. But move slowly and watch out for others."

"Gary . . . Gary . . . Gary . . ." Gary starts to say as he rotates. The sound is obvious when he takes his third turn. The echo isn't that loud, but if you know what to listen for, you can catch it. I hear him sliding away from me.

I hear others starting to move. Dean is saying his name and shuffling toward the mysterious wall, and I start to shuffle that way as well.

"John . . . John . . ." one voice says, turning.

"I'm also John," another voice says. "Small world."

"Not really," the first John says.

They share a laugh. It is a weird sound given our situation.

"Jerry . . . Jerry . . . Jerry . . . Jerry . . . Jerry . . . Jerry . . ." a voice says. Each time he says it he seems more concerned.

"Jerry, I think you are just a few feet away from me, and I just found my wall. Come toward the sound of my voice," one of the Johns says.

"Thank you." The relief in Jerry's voice is palpable.

"Oh God!" the other John shouts.

"What is it?" I ask.

"There is a body here."

"It's not the one Dean moved." I pause. "Unless he slung that son of a bitch across the room?"

Dean grunts. "No, he is over there." I can't see him pointing, but I know he is.

"Ben, that's not your guy, is it?" I ask.

"No, my guy is still here."

"Okay. John, can you tell if your guy is breathing?"

"Assuming it is a man," Dean says.

"Yeah, *he* is breathing," John says, putting a little emphasis on the pronoun.

"Great, so we are up to ten," I say.

"Yeah, ten," Ben says.

"What the fuck?" Dean interrupts.

"What is it?" I ask.

I'm not far from him, and I can hear his voice bouncing off the wall. Then I hear something else bounce off the wall. It is either Dean's foot, or he has a hand like a sledgehammer. The sound it makes is hollow, a deep rumbling sound.

"Is that glass?" I say as I approach the wall with my hand outstretched.

"Feels like it. Really fucking thick glass," Dean says.

My fingers touch it. It is cold. I knock just a little on it and listen as the echo rolls upward. I flinch as another sound pierces the darkness. I cover my ears. Someone is screaming.

"What the fuck is going on? I can't see anything! Who's there?" the screaming voice cries after he stops wailing. It sounds like the guy near Ben.

"Hey, hey, hey, calm down, you're okay," I say.

"Well, let's not go that far," Dean says.

"Hey, can you hear me?" I say to the newly awakened person.

"Who are you? What is happening?"

"My name is Crispin, and we haven't really figured out what is happening yet."

And, to make matters worse, the scream seems to have woken one of the others.

"Where am I? Why can't I see? Help!" a new voice yells. I think it's the person near Dean. "Help me!"

I hear a quick movement, and the voice is muffled.

"Shut the fuck up and we will explain everything," Dean growls.

"Everyone just calm down, okay? Cool it," I say. "If you just woke up, I want you to listen to me, okay?"

"What is going on?" the guy by Ben asks.

"I will explain everything we know if we can all just calm down for a moment, all right?"

I notice something then. The water has stopped pouring. It's too calm.

"Dean?" I ask.

"I'll let go of your neck if you can promise to be quiet and listen. Got it?" he says. There is a small gasp and Dean stands up. "Good. So we don't know what is happening. We all woke up down here and we don't know why."

After he says this I hear something far above us. It feels impossibly far away. I think the ceiling must be forty or fifty feet above us.

"Maybe Crispin should explain?" Gary says, and the water begins pouring again.

"Fuck you, John," Dean yells.

"That's Gary," one of the Johns says.

"Well, fuck you too."

"Okay, everyone just calm down," I say again. "So we don't know much, but we know that we all woke up down here and none of us remember being knocked out. It is dark as hell in here and no one can see anything. We've managed to get to what we believe are the four walls of the room, one of which we think is very thick glass. We haven't found a door yet, but that is the next step. Okay?"

"Where are we?" one of the new voices asks.

"We don't know yet," Ben answers.

"Were we in an accident?" the other new voice asks.

"No, it doesn't seem like that's the case. Last we remember we were all in separate locations," I say.

"And only men were taken," one of the Johns says.

"Taken? What do you mean, *taken*?" one of the new men cries.

"We don't know if we were taken, we don't know how we got here yet. But it does seem like we were placed here," I say.

"Placed here? By who?" he shouts.

"Again, we don't know that. We only know what I've just said." I consider this and add, "And that water is pouring in from somewhere way above us."

"I *thought* I heard water," Ben says.

"What the fuck did you think it was?" Dean snarls.

"Cool it," I say. "It is water, and it isn't draining. But it isn't even deep enough to accumulate across the room yet. So stay out of the middle and you will be fine for now."

"For now?" the person Dean had been choking asks.

"There is a grate in the floor," Dean says. "It is draining there."

"No, that drain is closed," I say. "Which means if we don't figure out what is going on, and that water keeps coming, we all may be taking a little bath if there isn't anywhere for it to go. So, if you don't mind, I would like to get moving ahead in finding a way out of here."

"What do we do now?" Ben asks.

"First off, the two of you who just woke up, what are your names?" I ask.

"Mike," the guy near Ben says.

"Great, and you?" I say.

"He is talking to you," Dean says, and there is a small thud.

"Terry," a small voice replies.

"Okay, Mike and Terry. I don't want to waste time with introductions, so I am just going to continue, is that okay?"

"Yeah," Mike says.

"I guess," Terry says.

"Great. Ben, can you help Mike up to the wall?" I ask.

"Yeah, I got him."

"Terry, you are at the glass wall with Dean and me. Can you stand?"

There is some shuffling and then he replies, "I'm up."

"Okay, it sounds like we have at least one person on every wall, correct?" I ask the room, and I'm met with a smattering of agreement.

"I think I am the only one over here."

"Okay, Gary, is that you?" I ask, almost certain that it is him.

"Yeah, it's me," Gary says.

"Great. Now, everyone stand against the wall. Gary, you stay where you are. Everyone else move, with your hands on the wall, toward each other until you are all together." I move the few feet until I bump into Dean.

"Make sure you are feeling the wall for anything at all. It can be a light switch, a door, a window, anything."

"What do you want me to do?" Gary asks.

"Just hang out, Gary," I say. "Let me know when everyone is together."

"We are," Ben says. "It's just the two of us."

"Awesome," I say.

"Two Johns and a Jerry over here," Jerry says. "All set. Now what?"

"Now, you're going to move apart again, in opposite directions. Keep moving along the wall, feeling your way around again, until you get to the corner. I'll go to my left and get to the corner, and whoever goes to their right of the John and Jerry group will get to their corner, then we will work our way in until we get to Gary. That'll mean we have covered the entire room."

"We will find the door for sure," Ben says.

"Unless it is a hidden door and we can't feel the seam," Dean says.

"Well, yes, that is a possibility," I say. "Now, before you start I want you to each count how many steps you go from where you are. You may not be right in the middle, but if we count we can add them up and get a good idea about just how big this place is. Okay?"

"Got it."

"Okay."

"Yep."

"Okay, Gary, stay put. I'm heading your way," I say as I take my first step, but the sound it makes forces everyone to stop what they are doing. The sound at any other time would be innocent and ignored. A minor annoyance at most. It is the slapping sound of stepping onto a wet surface.

"Oh shit," Gary says from the wall to my left. "Does that mean the water is rising?"

"We are going to drown," Jerry says.

"I can't swim," one of the Johns says.

"Everyone just calm down. This is why we need to find the door. We have a long time before it fills to any level that we need to be concerned with," I say, but neglect to include the fact that the water is pouring at a much faster rate now, and I know that soon the sound will be a roar in this echo chamber. "Everyone, keep moving. Except you, Gary—you stay put."

Everyone begins moving again. Most footfalls sound dry at first, but slowly they start to sound more and more wet. After a moment of everyone moving, Gary calls out.

"Ah, who is that?" he says in his typical whiny voice.

"It's me. Jerry."

"Sorry, you startled me," Gary says.

"I startled myself," Jerry says.

"I'm almost to you," I say, sliding my hand across the smooth steel wall. "Okay, I am here, Gary." I reach out and find Gary.

He pats my hand. I can tell his hand is shaking. "Gary, I need you to show me where the other person is. The one who is still out. We need to get him sat up against the wall so that he doesn't drown in just a few inches of water."

"Oh, he's right here." Gary takes my hand and pulls me just a foot or so from the wall. I can feel a body there. His chest is rising and falling slowly.

I am able to find his arms and get him pulled up against the wall. Part of me hopes he wakes up so we have one less thing to deal with, but I am aware that our clock is ticking and I don't want to take the time right now to explain what is happening.

"Get the fuck off me!" Dean says from the opposite side of the room.

"Calm down," Mike says. "I was just looking for the corner."

"Well, it feels like you're trying to grab my dick."

"Get over yourself," Mike says.

"I counted about fifteen steps," Ben says. "Probably twenty-five or thirty feet from where I was. Mike?"

"I had about ten steps," Mike says. "Maybe fifteen feet or so."

"Okay, so that's about, what, thirty feet?" I say.

"More like forty," Ben says.

"Right, yeah, sorry," I say. Math was never my strong suit, and I am more focused on the fact that the icy water is now starting to come up over the top of my shoe. "Officer Kurds, how many steps did you have to your corner?"

"Thirteen."

"So maybe like twenty to twenty-five feet?" I say.

"Yeah, sounds about right." His voice is a bit softer. If he is a cop, I suspect he is now catching on to the seriousness of this situation.

"Okay, I had eleven to my corner," I say. "So it sounds like this room is a square, can we agree on that?"

"Seems like it," Ben says.

"Yeah," Dean agrees.

"Likely," Gary says.

"Okay, anyone find anything on the walls?" I ask.

"Don't you think one of us would have said something if we had?" one of the Johns asks.

"Well, I would certainly hope so," I say.

"We need to see if anyone else is in here," Dean says. "We can't have anyone drowning."

"I think a few of us should keep searching for the door, and the rest start crisscrossing the room," I say.

"Maybe we should try to break the glass," Terry says.

"That's not glass. It's acrylic, and it's at least a foot thick. You ain't doing shit to that," Dean says.

"Well, no one else is doing anything," Terry cries. I try not to take offense.

"Terry. It's Terry, right?" I say.

"Yes."

"Terry, if we can find something strong and sharp to use to focus the force on a single spot, we may have a chance. Can you think of anything?"

"I don't have anything!" he whines.

"Okay, okay. Well, just keep that in mind in case we come across anything," I say.

I can hear Terry start beating on the glass in his frustration. The echo is deafening mixed with the sound of the water pouring in.

"Knock it off," Mike says.

"Shut up! We need to get out of here!" Terry shouts, and continues to bang on the glass.

"Quit your fucking bitching, and stop that fucking banging," Dean demands.

"Go fuck yourself. Who put you assholes in charge anyway?" Terry shoots back.

"Stop it," Dean says with a grunt.

Water sloshes, and the banging stops temporarily. The room goes quiet. The water has stopped running. The only sound is a struggle.

"Dean, stop," I say.

"This little fucker is pissing me off. I'm not going to keep listening to this. He is interfering with an investigation. I am placing him under arrest," Dean says.

"Get the fuck off of me," Terry says.

Then there is a wet slap. I don't have to see it to know what happened.

"Did you just fucking hit me?" Dean growls.

"Guys, the water has stopped. Can we just calm down?" I say.

The struggle sounds intense. I start to move that way, and then there is a loud thud as something hits the glass.

"Get him off of me!" Terry yells. "Help!"

I move faster. There is another thud. And another. Terry goes quiet. Two more thuds. I run into the glass just to the side of where the sound is coming from. I reach out and something soft and wet brushes my arm with some force before another thud. I hear a crack, but it isn't the glass.

"Dean, knock it off! You're going to kill him!" I shout. I grab for him.

"Get the fuck back," Dean says, shoving Terry's limp body into me. Dean is incredibly strong and I am forced backward, stumbling under the weight of the body being pushed into me.

I fall and Terry crashes down on top of me. I roll and toss him to the side, trying to get to my feet before Dean can grab me, but

I am too slow. I'm picked up by my shirt. I am again surprised by his sheer strength.

"Get your fucking hands off me," I growl.

He pushes me up against the glass. I can feel that his hands are trying to go to my neck. My fist thrusts forward between his arms and finds his chin. It gives a little, and his grip loosens for a split second. My feet come up and I put them both in his gut and push as hard as I can, using the glass to brace myself. Dean stumbles back and lets go of me. There is a splash as he falls into the water. He must have tripped over Terry.

"Motherfucker!" Dean yells.

"Stop!" I yell. "Listen!"

There is calm for a moment. A rumbling below us. Then a squeal.

"What is that?" Gary cries.

What follows as the water starts to move is the unmistakable sound of a tub draining.

"The water is draining!" Ben says.

Then something that none of us were prepared for happens. A bright light clicks on above us. I have to put my arm across my eyes. I don't know if the light is even that bright but, since I have been in the dark for what feels like forever, it is blinding. A few cries of pain and joy accompany the light. I blink a few times and begin taking in my surroundings.

The first thing I see in front of me is Dean. He is a good five inches taller than I am and easily sixty pounds of muscle heavier. He wears a police uniform, but it is noticeably lacking a badge, and his duty belt is gone. He looks around the room with his hand shading his eyes from the light. Another glance around the room shows that it's about the size we thought it was. Other than the people we accounted for, and the grate in the floor, there is nothing in this giant room. I try to look up at the light. The ceiling is at least fifty feet above our heads, and three of the walls are solid steel all the way up. I turn and look at the glass wall that isn't glass. It is indeed at least a foot thick, but it is easy enough to see through. The room on the other side is identical save two small differences: the room on that side is completely dry; and there is a large canvas bag, filled with something, on the far side.

As I take in the glass, I notice the red streaks dripping down it. My eyes move quickly to Terry, but it is too late. The small man lying in the water is dead. It is obvious. His head has been cracked open and blood pulls away in the current like nightmare hair in a strong wind. His eyes are rolled back in his head as he lays there.

"You fucking asshole," I shout at Dean, who whips his head back toward me. It is as if we both forgot we were in the middle of a fight when the light came on.

"You," he snarls.

He charges at me and body checks me with the force of a subway train. I hit the glass hard and rebound back into him. He hits me with a quick flurry of punches to the stomach and ribs. I fall to the ground on my side, thankful that the water is gone as I watch the last of it, and some of Terry's blood, drip into the drain. Dean's hands grab my shirt to lift me up, but he stops when I speak again.

"What is that?" I say, trying my hardest not to breathe through what feels like broken ribs. I point a finger toward the drain—and the smoke now rising from it.

"What the fuck?" Gary says, stepping forward to look at the drain.

I watch as his knees buckle and his head tilts forward and then backward. He drops into a mound on the floor. Two other men—I assume it's Jerry and one of the Johns—drop as well. Then Dean lilts and falls forward. He hits the glass and slides to the ground. I try to cover my mouth, but the foul-smelling gas is too powerful. The outside of my vision darkens and again I am thrown into that all-too-familiar feeling of being unconscious.

"Chris, wake up!" I hear someone yelling in the distance. My head is pounding. I hear water pouring and my legs are wet.

My brain attempts to pull me back to reality, but my memory has its hooks in the past. Visions of my first time in prison, feeling like I was being unfairly punished. Not that I didn't deserve to be there. But feeling like the punishment didn't fit the crime.

"Chris!" I open my eyes. I am sitting up and someone is standing over me. "Thank God. I thought we lost you!" I think the man yelling in my face is Ben, if my memory is serving me correctly. He looks about how I thought he would, a smaller man with wire-frame glasses.

"His name is Crispin, you idiot," one of the Johns calls from across the room. "Like the guy from the *Back to the Future* movies."

Ben looks down at me. "Is that right?"

"Sort of," I say. "Crispin Glover was only in the first one. He was replaced by Jeffrey Weissman in the sequels."

"No, it was Matthew Modine in the sequels," someone else, maybe Jerry, says.

"No, that wasn't Matthew Modine. He did look like him though," I say.

"I'm pretty sure that was him."

"Let's check." Yelling over the water into the open room, I say, "Hey, Siri, was Matthew Modine in *Back to the Future II* and *III*?"

There is an echo and then it is quiet for a moment and everyone I can see turns their heads toward the ceiling as if waiting for the response. After a second I break the silence.

"That would have been cool if it worked, right?"

"This isn't a time for joking," Jerry says.

"You're right," I say, and try to stand. The water is starting to creep up my legs, and if I stand now I can hope to keep dry a little longer.

As I stand, pain darts through my insides like a razor and I am reminded of the punches that hobbled me. I stand straight and get my guard up, my head on a swivel, but I don't see Dean.

"He's over there," Ben says, pointing behind me.

I turn and look through the glass wall I was leaning on. There, on the other side of the glass, is Dean, leaning against the far wall. His room is dry as a bone. He is sitting with his back against the wall and the large canvas bag drawn up beside him. The bag is open, and food and bottles of water are spilling out. He has a shit-eating grin on his face. When he sees that I am looking at him, he sets the candy bar he has been eating in his lap, takes a swig from a water bottle, and flips me off.

"Fuck you!"

His voice is muffled, but I can hear it way better than I thought I should be able to with the thick glass, the distance, and the now roaring water pouring behind me. I look around, and it is like Ben is reading my mind.

"We think there's a speaker in the ceiling. We can hear him and he can hear us."

"How long was I out?" I ask.

"We aren't sure how long any of us were out, but you woke up about two minutes after Mike, and he was the last of us up. About four minutes after the water started running again."

"And Terry?" I look around.

"Gone."

"What do you mean, *gone*?"

"He isn't here."

I turn and scan the room, then scan Dean's side. He flips me off again.

I yell at him through the glass, "What happened?" He just holds up a hand to his ear as if he can't hear me, but I can hear my voice echoing on his side. The water is now up around my calves. "Come on, man. Did you see anything? Is there anything else over there?"

Dean licks chocolate from his fingers, drinks from another water bottle, and then tosses it away half empty. I watch as it bounces and drains its liquid onto the floor. I didn't realize how thirsty I was until I watch the water from that bottle pour out onto the floor. I look down at the water pooling up around me and wonder if it's safe to drink if need be.

Dean pushes himself up on the wall and saunters over to the glass to look at me. We stare at each other for a few uncomfortable moments, and then he looks around at the glass before locking eyes with me again. "Looks like you are fucked," he says, and taps on the glass.

I want nothing more than to punch that stupid look off his face.

"Crispin," Ben says, touching my arm. "We have to figure something out. The water level is rising faster and faster."

I stare at Dean for another moment.

"You see anything? You know anything about this?" I ask.

"Just that it's easier on this side," he says.

"Protect and serve, right?" I say.

"Fuck you, *Chris*," he says.

I turn back toward Ben and the rest of our group. There are eight of us left over here.

"Someone said they can't swim?" I say.

"*I* can't," one of the Johns says.

"Okay, stick with Ben and me, and we'll keep you afloat, all right?"

"Yeah. Yeah, of course," Ben says after a moment of hesitation.

John shuffles his way through the water toward us. He is a heavier man, but I don't think his weight will be much of an issue when we are trying to tread water. I will just have to make sure he keeps calm and on his back.

"John, just stay with us, okay?"

"All right, thank you," he says.

Before I can say anything else, our light goes out.

"Oh God!" someone yells in the semi-darkness.

"What the fuck?" I say.

The light is still on in Dean's half of the room. He is standing there squinting at the glass. "Ah, come on. How am I supposed to watch you fucking guys struggle if the light is off?"

I scan the room again to determine how well I can see using just his light, but it isn't great. I can see a few feet in front of me. Only John and Ben are within view.

"I think we should all group up," I say.

"Well, at least I can still hear you," Dean yells.

"Go fuck yourself, Dean," I shout. "Okay, let's group up."

I can hear people moving toward John and Ben and me, and slowly the other five people come into sight.

"What are we supposed to do?" Mike says.

"Did he kill that guy?" the other John asks.

Dean runs at the glass. "I didn't kill *nobody*. You shut the fuck up!"

I turn and get as close to the glass as I can, hoping he can see me. "His head was busted open, you ignorant fuck. What did you think happened to him?"

"I was calming him down. He was going to get one of us killed if I didn't shut him up. I obviously did something right, since I'm over here and you're over there."

"Ignore him. We need to think," I say, turning away. The water is at our chests, and John grabs my arm tightly. "It's going to be okay, John. Just relax, okay?"

"I can't swim," he reminds me.

"I know, buddy. We won't let you drown."

Just as I say that, the water starts to creep up his neck. He tilts his head back.

"He isn't going to make it," second John says.

"Shut up. Yes, he is," I say to second John, and then turn to first John. "I need you to lean backward as if you were laying on a bed, okay?"

"I'll sink," first John says.

"You won't. Just take a deep breath and lean back. I will hold you up, but you need to take up as much surface area as you can, got it?"

He looks scared but does as I say and leans back. I put a hand under him to steady him as he starts to sink. He flails his arms and tries to stand, dropping his head beneath the water.

"Help!" he yells.

"I've got you, you just need to trust me," I say. The water is now up to my chin, and I am holding John up so he can breathe. "I need you to try again."

"Just listen to him," Ben says. He and all the others are starting to tread water.

"Come on, buddy. We can do this," I say.

I kick my feet out of my boots so I can swim a little better. John takes a deep breath and leans back. I am treading water now as well, and I put my hand under John and press him upward so he doesn't drop below the surface.

"Good job, just like that. You're doing great, just don't move. Take small breaths and try to keep as much air in your chest as you can."

"You're doing great, John," Ben says.

"I can't hold you like this for long, so I need to reposition," I tell John. "I am going to lay out on my back as well, and I'm going to put my side into your back and wrap an arm across your chest, okay?"

"What if I sink?"

"If your head goes under, just hold your breath. But whatever you do, do not put your legs or hips down, okay? You need to stay laying as flat as possible."

Ben reaches over and puts a hand under John's back while I transition to the standard lifeguard rescue maneuver. Once I'm in position, Ben moves his hand.

"Good job," he tells John, and pats him on the shoulder before returning to his own treading-water routine.

"Everyone else doing okay?" I ask.

I look around and see that most of the others have moved out of sight and into the dark. I can hear them swimming, but I cannot see them. We are now a good few inches above Dean's head as he stands on the other side of the glass with his hands cupped around his face trying to see into our side.

"I'm struggling," second John says.

"Let go of me," Mike says.

"Help me!" second John yells.

"I said get the fuck—" Mike is cut off by the sound of his head dropping below the surface.

"I don't know if I can do this for long," Jerry yells.

"Stop it!" a voice yells. It sounds like Mike.

"I can't," second John yells.

"Everyone calm down," I say, and try to swim toward them, but with John in tow I am afraid to go too fast or he will dip below.

"Help!"

The voices are starting to blur together.

"Get off—" Another voice, cut off by gurgling.

"Hey!" I say. "Listen, the water has stopped!" It's easy to notice the lack of the roar now that the water has stopped pouring in, but the noise has been replaced with screams for help.

"I can't . . ." More gurgling.

"I said stop!" someone yells.

"Nooo—" someone starts to plead before being cut off.

"Stop it!"

"Let him up!"

"Help him!"

"Somebody help me!"

"Ben, can you help them?" I yell, but my voice is drowned out by the screams of the others.

Then the rumbling noise returns. There is a clunk deep beneath us, and the water starts to swirl, and the light once again comes on for our side.

"What's happening?!"

"The water is draining! Swim outward as far as you can! Stay away from the center!" I say as I try to turn with John. The water is draining so fast that it is creating a whirlpool, but I manage to stay away long enough for it to drain to a point where I can stand and hold on to John so he isn't pulled into the grate, where he could be pinned by the force and drown in the water rushing downward.

Once the water has all drained, I look around the room. Everyone looks exhausted. Everyone except second John. He lays on his side, his eyes open, staring in my direction on the grate. I rush to him and roll him onto his back. I lean down to check for breath, but there is none, so I start chest compressions.

"You killed him," Jerry says softly. I look up, continuing the compressions, and see he is talking to Mike.

"I did not," Mike returns.

"I saw you hold him down," Jerry says, pointing at the man I am currently trying to press life into.

"He was trying to pull me down!" Mike shouts.

I feel movement on my arm and look back down, hoping to see some sign of life from the other John, but instead I see that it is the gas once again billowing up from the grate I am currently kneeling on. I don't even have time to warn everyone before the darkness takes me again.

If my mind is forcing me to revisit a past trip to jail or prison every single time I pass out, I'm in for a long night. This time I'm in Essex County lockup. I think that was the third or fourth time I went in, if you count the few times in a county holding cell. Nothing serious, just wrong place, wrong time, wrong person.

This time I wake up first. I am sat up against the wall facing the glass partition this time. I rub my eyes to clear them and can see Mike and Dean, now both laying on the dry side. Both appear to be out cold. I stand and walk over to Ben, who is closest to me. He is sat against the wall as well. I give his shoulder a shake and his eyes open slowly. He looks around and then up at me.

"Damn," he says.

"I know," I reply.

"I was hoping it was a bad dream."

"Me too." I extend my hand and he takes it and I pull him to his feet.

The water begins to pour. It sounds like it is at a much faster pace.

"At least they sit us up so we have a chance to wake up before we drown," Ben says.

"I just wish I knew who *they* are," I say.

"And why they're doing this," Ben replies.

Ben goes one way and I go the other, and we wake up the other four left on our side of the tank.

"The other John is gone," I say.

Ben looks around while he is shaking Jerry awake and asks, "You think they take the dead ones?"

"Starting to look like it." I look over at Mike and Dean on the far side of their room, and as if I willed them awake, they both start to move.

"This is fucked-up," Ben says.

"You okay, big guy?" I ask John as I help him to his feet.

"What is going on here?" John asks, but I just shake my head.

"Did he kill him?" Gary asks. "I saw him push him under."

"I don't know. It was either that or he drowned when he got caught on the grate."

"No," Mike's voice comes over the speaker, and I turn to look at him. "I think it is obvious what happened."

"Is it?"

"Yeah. I shoved him under the water," Mike says. He turns and finds the canvas bag, flips the flap open, and reaches in for a bottle of water.

"You're a monster!" Jerry shouts.

Mike doesn't respond. He just removes the cap from the bottle and takes a long drink before flicking the cap at the glass. He takes a second long pull from the bottle, then empties it with a third.

"I held him under because it was him or me. I felt him struggling, and it was terrible, but as soon as he stopped fighting, as soon as his body went limp, the water started to drain."

Dean looks like he's thinking, then he speaks. "That makes sense. When I slammed what's-his-name's head against the glass, the water started draining as soon as I felt his skull crack."

"Fuck you both," I say.

"You don't get it, do you?" Dean says, coming up to the glass. "It's a test."

"A test for what?" Ben asks.

"To see if you have what it takes to survive."

"You mean a test to see if you are capable of murder," I say.

"Crispin," John says. "The water."

I don't have to look down to know that the water is already up to my knees. It is coming much faster now.

"Looks like we know who the obvious choice is next," Mike says, taking a second water bottle from the bag.

"Shut up!" I yell at him.

"Go to hell!" John yells, coming up beside me.

"He isn't wrong," Jerry says.

I turn to see him getting closer.

"We aren't killing anyone," I say. I push John behind me, putting myself between him and Jerry.

"If that's what gets this all to stop though . . ." Gary says.

"Stay away from me!" John yells.

"Everyone just be cool," Ben says.

"Yeah, be cool," I say.

It's too late. Gary and Jerry rush me. Gary is small but jumps and grabs at my face. I pivot and toss him to the side, but it opens me up, and Jerry, who is of medium build and clearly played football in high school, spear tackles me, shoving his shoulder right into my stomach. I can feel my damaged ribs scream out in pain as I fall backward into the water. I gasp for air and instead get a mouthful of the bitter-tasting water. I struggle to get to my feet, but someone is holding me back. I push backward, slamming whoever it is into the wall, and the pain in my ribs forces me to my knees again. The water is now so high that even on my knees I have to look up to breathe. When I do, I see Ben's sad eyes looking back at me.

"I'm sorry," he says.

The water has stopped pouring. I stand and see that Gary and Jerry each have one of John's arms pulled back and they have his head underwater. I try to move toward him, but Ben grabs me. I look to see the other man, the one who never told me his name, standing there looking at the scene.

"Help him, goddammit!" I yell, but the man just stands there. I pull against Ben, but the pain cripples me.

I hear the rumble, and the water begins to drain. As soon as it is low enough to sit, I do. I pull my shirt up, covering my nose and mouth in preparation for what I know will come next. John's lifeless eyes are looking right at me. Ben puts his hand on my shoulder as the gas begins flowing.

I look over and see Mike and Dean sitting against the wall sharing what appears to be a sleeve of cookies. Their faces disappear behind the gas flowing into their room. Ben sits down and leans against the wall. Seconds later his body goes limp. I am the last one awake, but it doesn't last long. I hear a noise above me and daylight shines in as the vault door high above is opened and a shadow lowers itself down into the chamber. Then I am gone again.

My sentence got extended when I was sup-posed to leave Essex County. I'm not saying I didn't deserve it. I'm not saying I don't deserve any of this. I'm saying that it was another situation where I feel like the system was rigged against me. Another time where moral choice maybe wasn't the legal choice.

When I wake I can hardly breathe. I am wheezing with every breath. Everything hurts. I have been sat up against a wall again and the water is coming quickly. It is cold and already up to my chest as I sit here. The cold makes the pain worse. I look around the room. The three of us remaining are spaced out. Ben sits across the room from me, the glass wall to my right. On the wall to my left is the man who just stood there not saying anything.

"Who are you?"

He doesn't respond. He just stares ahead at the glass wall as if he doesn't notice the water rising around him. Ben gives me a knowing look and then nods toward the silent man. I get what he is saying and I shake my head.

"Hey, guy, who are you?" I ask again.

No response.

I look over to the other room and see the four men there. They are just waking up. Not having the brutal awakening of the icy water, they stay down longer. I stand, and something falls from my lap and plunks down into the water. Ben also stands, but the other man does not move. He just continues to breathe deeply.

"What was that?" Ben shouts across the din of the water.

"I'm not sure," I shout back. I look down into the water, but it's too dark. I fish around with my foot in its waterlogged sock to see if I can find the item. Using my hands would be more effective, but the pain of bending over would make it impossible to breathe. I can hear the other men in the dry room stirring, and then Gary shouts something that causes my blood to freeze in my veins.

"Where did you get a knife?"

I turn and look over at the men on the other side. Dean is standing in the middle of the room holding a medium-size hunting knife. The other men back away from him, even though he is not holding the knife in a threatening way.

My mind works quickly to analyze the sound I heard when I stood. The size and shape of the knife Dean is holding would have made that sound as it fell into the water. I have to find it. I bend to plunge my hands into the water, but it's too late, I've lost my advantage, and something slams into me. The pain from my ribs reverberates throughout my body as I fall backward and am submerged completely. A foot kicks out and catches my leg. I try to stand, but a flurry of punches keeps me from getting my head above the surface. I manage to push myself away under the cover of the dark water. When I am free of the punches I quickly raise my head and gasp for air.

"Ben, help!" I cry, and it echoes off the walls now that the water has stopped.

I try to stand but cannot get my feet under me enough to do so. A kick sends me falling forward and as I do I see him. The man who refused to talk. He is standing right where he was when I woke up. He hasn't moved other than to stand. He still isn't looking at us. He just stares forward.

"Ben!" I cry out as I am forced under the water.

My lungs try for air and only find the cold embrace of what I fear will soon be death. I roll to my side and try to use my hands to push myself upward and away from my attacker. As I move, my hand brushes something. I realize it is my last chance, and even though I fear I am less than a second from drowning, I reach for it. My fingers curl around it and I swing my arm backward but hit nothing. Ben must have seen what I'm holding because he has moved back. I stagger to my feet.

"You don't have to do this, Crispin," Ben pleads. "Look, I wasn't going to kill you if I got the knife."

"Bullshit." Dean's voice booms over the speaker. "Kill his ass, Chris. Then you can come over here with us, and you and I can finish what we started." He taps the knife against the glass. The others stand behind him as if they are a gang and he is their leader.

"I'm not killing anyone," I say. Ben steps forward, and contrary to what I just said I lift the knife and back him up. "I won't kill you, Ben, but that doesn't mean I won't cut your fucking balls off if you touch me again."

"Take it easy, man. We can work together on this," he says, and looks over at the man against the wall again.

The water seems to stop when we are fighting, and I know I won't be able to defend myself against the two of them in my condition if I am also trying to swim, so whatever I'm going to do, I need to do it now before the water starts again.

"I won't kill anyone," I say again. "If you need to kill me then you can try, but just know that it won't be easy."

Ben looks over at the man against the wall. The water begins to pour again.

"I think he's blind," Ben says. "You just hold him and we'll both get credit."

The knife is out in front of me and Ben reaches for it.

"Just give it to me and I'll bring him over to you. You grab him and hold his arms."

"I'm not killing anyone," I say, and with a flick of my wrist I fling the knife through the air away from Ben. It splashes down and I see the man against the wall turn his head toward the sound.

"What the fuck, man!" Ben turns to go for the knife and I fall against the wall.

The pain and cold wrap around me and I feel the lights dimming again. The water stops and I can hear a struggle. I don't want to see what is happening, so I bury my head into my arm and lean against the wall. The struggle is fairly brief and ends with a tearing and a guttural scream. It takes all my strength not to fall face-first into the water. I push myself against the wall and wait for the drain to begin doing its work. Mercifully it does. I can hear someone moving around in the shallow water, but I don't have the strength to look. They don't sound like they are moving toward me, so I focus on staying awake long enough to lower myself to the floor once the water is gone. It doesn't work, and the black takes me.

I never felt like being inside rehabilitated me. I don't know that I deserved rehabilitation. I'm not saying I didn't commit crimes. I have. More crimes than I was ever convicted of, and by a long shot. But all but one of my crimes was in support of someone else. I stole to feed my nephew. I burglarized a store to make sure my sister could give him a Christmas. And I hurt the drunk driver who took him from her.

It's hard to open my eyes. Pain racks my body's every nerve. The water is pouring and is already up to my neck as I lean against the wall. I can just sit here and let it take me. I lean my head back against the wall and just listen as I resign myself to my death. The water is loud, but I can hear something over it. Yelling, screaming. Arguing. I look over my shoulder and through the glass into the other room. There are a few inches of water pooled on that side of the room now. Ben is lying on the floor. He is bleeding from what appears to be a knife wound to the abdomen. I glance around my room and see I am alone. I stand and turn to watch as the water on my side climbs higher.

Dean stands in the middle of the room holding his knife. Mike, Jerry, and Gary surround him and move in a circle trying to get an angle on him. He swings the knife wildly at them.

"Just put the knife down and let's see what happens when he dies," Jerry says, nodding to Ben.

"And risk waking up with one of you fucks having the knife? No thanks," Dean says.

The water lifts me and I lay back, spreading myself out as much as I can. I take a deep breath. It hurts like a son of a bitch, but I hold most of it in and allow myself to float. The water is rising quickly and I focus on the single light high above my head as I am drawn closer to it.

The sounds of the fight below me ricochet off the walls. It sounds like Dean has stabbed someone else.

"Why didn't the water drain?" Mike calls out. "Ben is dead, and Jerry's nearly there!"

Mike's voice is silenced, and the struggle continues.

It is a strain to stay conscious as I float here in this tomb. I know if I pass out I'll sink and that will be it for me, and I know that is inevitable, but I can't bring myself to allow the darkness to have me yet.

Then I see it. Above me, just to the side of the light, is the hatch I saw opened before. There is a lever on it that says *Pull to Exit* and I am getting closer to it. I reach my hand up and try to summon it to me.

The fighting continues, now forty feet or so below me. The water continues to rise. The handle is just ten or so feet away. I am even closer when the water stops pouring. I reach up as far as I can, but it is just out of my grasp. With the movement I sink a little and drop below the surface. It takes all of my will power to get myself afloat again.

"What the fuck is going on here?" Dean yells. His voice is deafening now that I am so close to the speaker and the sound has nowhere left to go in this now waterlogged room.

"Shut up," I say, and I can hear my voice echo in his chamber.

"You're still alive?" Dean calls out.

"Barely."

"Well then, it's just you and me."

"Is that so?" I say, reaching up for the handle as if my arm grew another few inches in the last few minutes.

"Why'd my water stop, and why isn't it going down?" Dean asks. I don't know if he is asking me, or whomever is behind this, or maybe it's rhetorical, but I answer.

"Go fuck yourself."

"*You* go fuck yourself," he replies.

"Very clever comeback," I say, reaching up again and nearly going under the water for my trouble.

"What am I supposed to do?" he yells, and again I don't know if he is talking to me. I choose not to reply this time.

The outside of my vision is starting to go dark and my lungs are burning. I know I can't keep myself awake much longer.

"Chris? You still there?"

I try to respond but I can't.

"Chris? Chris? Are you there?"

The terror in his voice is both pathetic and sad. If I didn't hate him I would feel sorry for him.

"Crispin?" he says.

I can feel the anger flow through me. The selfishness in that word. Only when faced with death is he willing to call me by my name. I use the anger and take the deepest breath I can and push myself under the surface. I swim down as far as my broken body will allow. I can just barely make out Dean's upturned face looking at me from his side. Then I turn, pointing myself upward at the hatch, and kick as hard as I can toward the surface. I breach and shoot my arms up. My right hand hits the handle, but I can't grab it. Luckily my left hand manages to snag the very end of it. I summon everything I've got and swing my other hand back up to give it a pull.

There is a metallic clang and the handle is ripped from my hands as the hatch flips upward with considerable force. The water seems even colder as I am plunged back into it.

"What is that? Is that a door?" Dean yells.

I swim wildly, trying to get my head back above the water, when my hand catches something hard. Once my head is clear of the water I can see it. It is the rung of a chain ladder that has dropped from the opening. It only hangs down about a foot past the top of the water, but it is enough for me to pull myself up with.

"Crispin! You can't leave me down here!"

I lift myself out of the hole and flop onto the dirt next to the opening. I am in the middle of the woods and I can't see anything but trees in any direction. I lay on the ground looking up at blue sky and listening to Dean yell in the hole. There is another hatch a few feet away that presumably goes to his side. I contemplate who put us there. What they used to get down there and move us. That wasn't my first time in a cell, but I don't ever plan on going back. I think about my nephew and the decision I made to drive that night. Was this my punishment? Was this my rehabilitation? My mind wanders to what they were trying to learn from this, or what they were trying to teach us, as the world slowly slips away and I fall once again into darkness.

BURY MY BODY SOMEWHERE NICE

Part One: The Body

Shadows of trees against the inky sky hold the shoulder as if giant hands securing the winding road to the side of the mountain. The pass above Black Hawk is beautiful during the day, but at night any road up in the high country of the Rocky Mountains can be treacherous. I've been up this way a few times after dark, but tonight my nerves are a ball of rubber bands sitting high in my throat. I made the drive just last week to make sure I could find the turnoff, but now, faced with having to find it in the pitch-black, with only the lights of my Jeep to guide me, I am struggling.

"Did I pass the bridge?" I ask, not expecting an answer. "I know the turnoff was past the bridge."

"But which bridge?" asks a voice from the back.

I scream. I can't help it. I also jerk the wheel, which in a Jeep Wrangler is apt to get you killed. Thankfully no one is coming as I fly across the opposing lane and slide the vehicle to a stop on the small gravel shoulder on that side of the road.

My knuckles are like little white skulls staring back at me from the top of the steering wheel. I wait, my breath barbed into my ribs like thousands of fishhooks in my chest. I'm waiting for the inevitable blow to the back of my head. I shouldn't have left the tire iron back there. I knew better.

"Hey, you okay up there?" the voice asks.

I turn my head, not wanting to look, but I need to. I know when I do he'll be sitting there, free from the tarp I wrapped him in, blood still running from his head, with that same tire iron I used on him in his hand, ready to repay the favor.

It's dark, but I can still see well enough in the moonlight coming through the window. He's still there, right where I left him. I'd pulled the rear seat out of my little two-door Jeep so that I could fit a body back there. It was still tight, but by bending his legs I was able to cram him in. I'd put a painter's plastic drop cloth in and then laid the tarp on top so when I put the body in I could wrap the tarp around it like a corpse burrito. His head seems to have jostled enough to pull the tarp away from his face, so I can see him clearly in the moonlight. The side of his head is completely caved in. The skin has peeled around his scalp like old wallpaper and there is a clear line of sight past his busted skull right into his mangled brain. One of his eyes is open but rolled back into his head; the other is looking straight down, barely hanging on to whatever in there holds it in place.

I look around, expecting to see someone else in the car with me, but there's no one there. It's just us.

"What the fuck?" I ask myself.

Then it happens. A *sloppy* noise. Like thick fingers digging a ball bearing out of a tub of Vaseline. When I look back at him a second time, both eyes are fixed squarely on me.

"Jesus Christ!"

I grab for the door handle and throw myself out into the night.

"Come on, man. That's just rude," the voice calls from inside the Jeep.

"Shut up!"

I walk a few steps up the road, the headlights casting my shadow along the rocky face of the mountain.

"Fuck!" I yell into the night. "How is this fucking guy still alive?"

I look back toward the Jeep, expecting him to be sitting up in the back, but he's not.

"How the fuck is he still alive?"

The anger of the situation catches up with me and I can feel adrenaline tickle the back of my neck.

"How in the fuck is this motherfucker still alive?"

This time, I feel like I'm someone else. Someone much more confident. I feel like the guy who planned and carried out a murder.

"Attempted!" the voice calls from the back of the Jeep.

"What the fuck did you just say?" I yell, not realizing he answered something I didn't actually ask.

I sprint to the back of the Jeep, ready to finish the job I started at the rest stop.

"Okay, motherfucker, I've had—" I start, but my big moment is spoiled by the fact that I've locked the tailgate of the Jeep. "Dammit."

After retrieving the keys from the ignition I return, ready to do it, but I admittedly have lost a little of the gumption I had before, and pull the door open with a little more trepidation than I planned. If he were sitting back there with the tire iron he would have been able to get the drop on me, but he isn't. He's still wrapped up in the green tarp, right where I left him. He's still facing the front, so I have a clear look down at the left side of his head, the side I'd collapsed.

His eyes turn toward me again, his head not moving at all.

"You cool, bro?" he asks.

"Don't call me 'bro,' " I say, reaching in and grabbing the tire iron from where it had slid down between his legs and the back of the driver seat.

"I'm sorry, bro, what would you like me to call you? I never exactly got your name when you rushed me at the rest stop."

"You know who I am," I say.

"Wait," he says, eyeing me up and down the best he can with his head still facing the front. "Keegan? I thought you said you were fourteen?"

The tickle of adrenaline returns and I jam the pointed end of the tire iron, the one used to pry off hubcaps, into the gap between his skull and directly into the mushy flesh of his brain.

"Bro!" he yells.

The sound of his voice sends me stumbling back, the tire iron still buried in his cracked melon.

"Not fucking cool, bro," he says.

I step forward and swirl the tire iron to the best of my ability. It's like trying to stir thick dough. It doesn't move at first, but with enough wiggling I get some motion. After a minute of stirring his brain stew I step back, pulling the tire iron out and throwing it on top of his body. I fight the urge to spit on him. I'm not angry enough to purposefully leave DNA on someone I just murdered.

"You done?" he asks.

"What the fuck?" I shout. "Why won't you die?"

"What are you talking about? I'm very clearly dead as shit, bro."

"Stop calling me 'bro'!"

"You think I have a choice in the matter? Ha, *matter*, like brain matter, get it?"

"What?"

"I'm only saying *bro* because you assume I'm the type who would," he points out.

This makes sense. I'm losing my mind. I've snapped.

"What's your name?" I ask.

"Derrick," he says without hesitation.

"That your real name?"

He looks at me with an eyebrow raised.

"Right," I continue. "You wouldn't know that because I don't know that."

"I may have a wallet," he says. "Unless I left it in my car back at the rest stop."

I contemplate it. Is knowing this guy's name important enough to go rooting around on his corpse to find out?

"You'll know eventually, either way. Once my car has sat in the lot long enough, someone will wonder where I went. Then, when they can't find me at home, it'll be a news story."

Light breaks around the corner and a car comes flying down the mountain toward me. It looks like a luxury SUV of some sort. Probably too big to be going that fast down the mountain. They see my headlights on the side of the road and slow down.

"Fuck," I say under my breath. "You stay quiet."

I toss the tarp back over Derrick's head and slam the Jeep tailgate right before the

SUV pulls off the road and comes to a stop right behind my Jeep. I wipe my hands on my pants like I was doing some sort of manual labor.

An older man gets out of the driver's side and is followed by a younger man from the passenger's side.

"Good evening!" I say, trying to seem as calm as I can without being too memorable.

"Smooth," Derrick's voice says. It comes through muffled from behind the back window, but it's there.

"Evenin'," the older of the two say. "Everything okay?" He nods to the Jeep.

I use this to my advantage and turn over my shoulder to look in the back window and make sure Derrick is covered. Thankfully he is.

"Don't sweat, bro. I'm snug as a bug in a rug in here," Derrick says.

"Oh, yeah," I say, looking back at the man. "I had a wheel sensor flashing at me, so I needed to check them. All good though. I think the wire just came loose."

This is a lie, but a good lie. Anyone who has owned a Jeep Wrangler knows that stupid sensor wire gets worn and torn all the time.

"I had that same problem with my Wrangler," the younger man says. "Easy fix and you can order the replacement online. Shouldn't be a problem until then, as long as you don't mind the flashing light."

"You really out there lying to these fine folks?" Derrick yells from the back. From their lack of reaction it is obvious they can't hear him.

"Yeah, it's annoying," I say to them, "but as a Jeep owner, when *isn't* a light flashing at us from the dashboard?"

"I know that's right," the young man says.

"Kinda late to be going up the mountain," the old man says, ignoring the rapport the young man and I are building.

"I bet it's his dad," Derrick yells. "You've got the son on your side, but Pops isn't buying it."

"I'm, uh—my girlfriend and I are camped up the road a bit, and I had to run down to get more firewood," I say.

"Oh, come on now," Derrick interrupts. "It's one thing to murder a man and lie about it. But to lie about having a girlfriend? You're better than that."

"It's a red day," the old man says, acting like I should know what this means.

"Come on!" Derrick says. "You knew to pay attention to the fact that there was a campsite up there, just in case someone asked you what you were doing up here, but you don't know what a red day is? I mean, I don't either, obviously, but I'm also not the mastermind here."

"A red day?" I ask.

"Fire advisory," he explains. "You can't have a campfire tonight, son."

"Oh!" I say. "Right! I knew that."

"Thankfully it ain't supposed to be too cold tonight," the young man says.

"You all got enough blankets and sleeping bags up there?" the old man asks.

"Oh yeah, I've got a bunch of blankets," I say.

"And a tarp!" Derrick shouts. If they could hear him, they would have then, but they don't move.

"Well, okay then," the old man says. "Be safe up there."

"Have a good night," the young man follows.

The two get back in their car and just like that they are on their way down the mountain again.

I get back in the Jeep and pull back onto the road, heading once again toward my destination.

"That was close," Derrick says.

"Shut up," I say.

"I'm just saying, you didn't really play that too cool back there."

"It didn't help that you wouldn't stop talking," I say, realizing how stupid that sounds.

"So, what's our plan now?" he asks.

"I have the perfect spot to hide a body," I say.

"Oh? Do you now?"

I spot the trail I've been looking for. It's overgrown, but I see it cutting off the road and disappearing into the void that is the woods.

"I do. I found it out here a few years ago when I was hiking with my buddy Clint," I say, a smirk coming across my face.

"What makes it the perfect spot?"

"It's a spot where the rock face of the mountain seems to have shifted, and there is a hole that goes down probably like sixty feet. It's narrow, but if you can get the body down there it looks like it drops into an underground river. Clint said that the water probably goes to an underground basin or something. A body going down there is gone forever."

"How narrow?" he asks.

"What?"

"How narrow is the hole? I suspect I'm a little wider around the midsection than you anticipated."

He's right. I was worried about it the second I saw him at the rest stop. The photos he'd sent me when I was talking to him on the Internet, pretending to be a teenage boy, showed him as a much younger, much thinner man. In those photos he was maybe one hundred sixty-five pounds. Now he's closer to two twenty.

"You'll fit," I say.

"When was the last time you went out to this hole? Is it still there?"

"Where would it have gone?"

"Shit, I don't know. But if *I'm* asking, you clearly must be thinking about it."

He's not wrong. I wanted to go up to the hole, but instead I just drove by the turnoff a bunch of times. Then, about a week ago, I drove down the road to make sure it was still clear and nothing was going to get in my way, but I didn't want to be seen up by the hole, so I didn't make it that far. Last thing I need now—besides a dead guy talking to me—is a tree down across the path with that dead guy still in the back of my Jeep.

"It'll be there." The power of positive thinking at work.

"So what came first, the decision to kill me, or the discovery of the hole?"

"What do you mean? I found that hole years ago. I just met you a few weeks ago."

"Right, but did you decide to kill me and then you were like, 'Shit, I know just where I can hide the body!' " he says. "Or was it more like you found the hole, decided it was the perfect place to hide a body, and you've been looking for a victim ever since?"

"Hey, cool it with the 'victim' stuff," I interject. "You're a fucking pedophile."

"Am I?"

"Yeah, you are. You were ready to hook up with me if I was a fourteen-year-old boy. You were willing to let a fourteen-year-old boy hitchhike out to a rest stop in the middle of the mountains, alone, and meet up with you. You're disgusting."

"Okay. And you're certain it's me?"

My mouth falls open. I was trying not to let the doubt creep out of the place I'd hidden it in my brain. I say nothing.

"How closely did you look at me before you swung that tire iron? Because, if I re-member correctly—and keep in mind my brain is currently leaking all over the back of your Jeep, so my memory might not be the strongest—but I recall getting back to my car after using the bathroom, and you were parked next to me. You got out, called me Derrick, and then swung. Did you even look around before you did it?"

"I did look around, there was no one else there. And you answered when I called you Derrick," I accuse. I stop the Jeep on the hidden road and twist in my seat to see him. "You said your name was Derrick."

"Did I?"

"Didn't you?"

"Did I have time before you fucking clobbered me?"

"Okay, now you're just being dramatic."

"You killed me without knowing if I was actually the person you were looking for, and *I'm* the one being dramatic?" he counters.

"I checked for an ID, but you didn't have your wallet."

"Of course I didn't. I just went to piss."

"But you're Derrick, right?"

"Am I?"

I pull my phone down from the holder on the dash and click away from the navigation screen to look for the photos he sent.

"You have your navigation on?" he asks.

"Yeah, why?"

"To the place you plan to hide a body?"

"Shit."

I click back over to the navigation, take one last look at where I need to go, then stop the route.

"You're really not good at this."

I find the photos in my secure folder and pull up one of his face. I hold it up to compare, but it's too dark. I click on the phone's flashlight.

"Fuck, warn a guy before you do that," Derrick says, closing his eyes.

There's too much damage. It's impossible to tell if it is the same person. There are things that look similar, but nothing specific enough. I scroll through the photos and then find it. A photo he sent me of his dick.

There is a pretty good-size mole at the base of his shaved shaft.

"Wanna see?" he says, and winks at me.

"Fuck," I say, turning off the flashlight and throwing the phone into the passenger seat.

I start to drive again. The navigation app said it's just a few more minutes up the road to where I need to stop and find the trail-head.

"So?" Derrick asks.

"So what?"

"Did you kill me just because you found the perfect spot to hide a body?"

"I killed you because you were a fucking pedophile."

"Allegedly."

"It's you. Okay? Just shut up and let me drive. It's hard enough to see out here without you talking." I squint into the darkness outside the headlights, looking for the break in the trees that signals the path up to the rocks.

"So cliché," he says, breaking the silence I requested.

"What is?"

"You. This. Every fucking person ever claims they have the perfect place to hide a body. Everyone. And you think somehow yours is the ultimate one."

"Hey, fuck you, okay? There are probably bodies hidden all over these mountains, and none of them will ever be found. Including yours, fucker."

"I'm just saying, your spot may not be as good as you think it is."

"Well, we're about to find out," I say as I pull the Jeep off onto the trailhead going up to the rocks. "We're here."

"Yippie," he replies with zero enthusiasm.

When I open the back of the Jeep, his eyes are open again and he is looking at me. It's dark, but the light in the Jeep is enough to see him clearly. The blood from his head is pooled under him, and a little has gotten on the drop cloth, but nothing has made it to the Jeep's interior.

"Good thinking with the second layer of protection," he says. "You really have been planning this for a while."

"Shut up."

Standing here in the dark, I realize I may not be strong enough to carry him all the way up to the hole.

"That extra weight you weren't anticipating is really biting you in the ass now, isn't it?" he asks, snapping his jaw closed and clacking his teeth.

"I've been carrying around a few bags of dog food at home trying to prepare for it. But I thought you were smaller."

"Or you have the wrong guy."

"I don't have the wrong guy!" I yell.

"You sure about that?"

I turn away from him, not wanting to face that accusatory look.

"The mole," I say.

"The what?"

I pull open the tarp and grab at his belt buckle.

"Okay, now we're talkin'!" he says. I think I feel his hips press up into my hands, but I ignore it.

"Shut up," I say, pulling open his pants. He's wearing white cotton briefs.

"Are those the underpants of a pedophile?" he asks. "Don't answer that."

I take a deep breath, unable to believe what I am about to do, and then pull his shorts down. His stomach is hairy, and that hair trails all the way down to a thick patch of hair surrounding a very flaccid penis.

"Well, doc? Is it a boy?" he asks.

"You were shaved in the photo."

"I could have let it grow back."

The contents of my stomach must know what I'm thinking before I do, because they race up my throat and I have to choke them back.

"I have to look," I say, swallowing the bile and McDonald's chicken sandwich that threatens to escape.

"Have at it."

I push the hair aside and examine the base of his penis.

"Have you rooted out zee mole yet, 007?" he says, inflecting a horrible accent.

I let his underwear snap back up and cover him with the tarp again.

"Fuck."

There is silence for a moment. The sounds of the high country at night creep in. Wind moans through the trees. A wild dog howls somewhere in the distance. The sound of a car going past on the main road a few miles away echoes off the rocks.

"You have to do it. You know that, right?" he finally says, breaking the silence.

"I could just take you back to town and turn myself in," I reply.

"You do that and *both* our lives are over."

I don't respond. I just stare off into the darkness.

"Come on, man."

Man. Not *bro. Man.*

"I can't."

The night sky is amazing up here. So many stars. There's so much beauty to be found when you get away from the city.

"You don't want to miss this," he says. "You turn yourself in and you'll never see this again."

"I never appreciated it before, so what big loss is it if I never see it again?"

"You ever seen *Fight Club*?"

"You know I have," I say.

The irony of me talking to myself about *Fight Club* is not lost on me.

"Tomorrow will be the most beautiful day of your life. Your breakfast will taste better than any meal you and I have ever tasted," he says, quoting a line in the movie about starting over.

"I killed an innocent man," I say.

"You don't know that. I could have been a total asshole."

"It's not illegal to be an asshole."

"It should be."

"Yeah."

I take in the sounds of the night and the stars splattered across the sky for a few more minutes. I think of my ex-girlfriend. How she treated me like shit when all I wanted to do was make her happy. How my jealousy drove us apart. How needy I was because I was so worried she'd leave me that it eventually drove her to do just that. I think about my mom, how she instilled those abandonment issues into me. Back to high school, when all I wanted to do was belong. To hang out after school. To sing anthem rock songs with friends while we cruised with the windows down. To be normal. Instead, I'm standing here in the middle of the night next to a dead man whose dick I just touched. Of all the directions I thought my life could go, this was not one.

"You've got no one," says the body in the back of my Jeep that may or may not be a man named Derrick, who is definitely a pedophile.

"Hey, thanks for pointing that out, pal," I reply. "I thought you were supposed to be talking me out of throwing myself headfirst down that hole up there?" I nod up the trail toward the hole.

"No, what I'm saying is that you've got no one else to worry about. You can just free yourself of my burden, head back to town, and start a whole new life tomorrow. I mean, look what you've done. You saw the perfect place to dump a body. You waited until you found the right mark, then you planned and executed. Literally and figuratively."

"But I killed the wrong person!" I kick at the dirt behind the car, sending pebbles flying into the trees and scaring some unseen animal into darting down the road in the direction I came.

"Sure, but like ninety-nine percent of your plan worked. That's not bad."

"I'd say more like fifty percent."

"Let's say ninety," he negotiates.

"But that's a big ten percent."

"You're telling me. That ten percent got my head stoved in."

"Sorry about that," I say.

"Hey, do me a favor and just get rid of my body, okay? There's no reason for you to keep suffering this thing. You feel bad enough."

"I'm going to feel guilty my entire life."

"I appreciate that, but I absolve you. I'd shake your hand if I could."

"I don't think that's how it works, but I appreciate it."

"If you're going to make it home before midnight, we better get moving," he says.

I pull out the flashlight I keep under the seat of the Jeep and shine it up the hill. The rocks are farther than I remembered, but there is a positive, finally.

"Looks like someone's driven up that path and knocked down the few little trees and bushes that blocked it."

"Looks like your luck is changing. Think you can get the Jeep up there? That'd save you having to carry me."

"Exactly what I was thinking," I say, swinging the tailgate shut and jumping back into the driver seat.

It only takes a minute to get up to the rocks, and I don't have to break my back carrying a body. I'm taking it as a sign I'm on the right path. The headlights illuminate the entrance to the hole and I can feel my heart rate increase. I've been waiting years to do this since I saw this hole.

"It's like a good box," the man says as I start to unload him from the back of the Jeep.

"What?"

"You know? When you get older and you see a good cardboard box and you have to keep it, because you know someday you will use that box and it will be so satisfying to have it."

"It's not like that at all," I argue.

"It's exactly like that. You saw a perfect hole and you wanted to fill it—"

"Don't be gross."

"I'd argue that you're the one being gross."

I ignore this and wrap the tarp back around his head. Once I've got him up on my shoulders, I cross the few steps to the top of the hole.

"Well, it's been interesting," I say, shifting his weight to drop him in.

Instead, I drop him onto the ground beside me.

"Fuck!" he says as he hits the ground.

"Fuck," I parrot.

Part Two: The Woman

"Okay. Fifty percent," he says from his place at my feet.

"Shut up," I say.

Just a few feet down in the hole, wedged between the rocks, is a woman.

"She dead?" not-Derrick asks.

The headlights provide a lot of light, but there isn't enough shining down the hole, so I grab my flashlight.

The woman appears to be around my age, maybe mid-twenties. Her dark brown hair is short and styled. It looks like she was out on a date, maybe. She's stuck down there feetfirst. The black dress she is wearing is pulled up to her waist, where her hips are stuck between the rocks. If it weren't for the odd angle of her head, and the bruising, I would say she was just sleeping, but more than likely someone strangled her then broke her neck for good measure.

"I think so," I say. "She's stuck."

"That little lady wouldn't fit down there, and you thought *I* was going to?"

"It looked bigger before," I explain.

"Well, get a stick or something and jam her down so we can get this show on the road."

"I can't do that!" The idea of damaging this woman's body more than someone already has makes me uneasy.

"You can't just leave her there."

"Why not?" I ask.

"Well, first off, if you don't move her then you can't try and get *me* down there. And if you can't get me down there, what are you going to do with me? And second, if you leave her there, and someone else finds her, you've got the two guys we ran into on the way up here to put you near the crime scene. Plus, you've got your tire tracks and footprints all the way up here. The cops will be at your door before you can say 'double homicide.'"

"Hey, I didn't hurt her," I say.

There is a heavy pause.

"That was a weird way to say that," he says.

"I mean I didn't *kill* her. I wouldn't have done that," I say.

"Did it or not, you're on the hook for it. You can't really say you just stumbled upon her like that."

"Sure I can."

"And what exactly will you tell them you were doing up here?"

"Shit."

Sweat beads up on my palms and I begin to hyperventilate. This has been one failure after another and I just can't take it. There is a ledge just a few feet away. It wouldn't take much to just toss myself over.

"Take a few deep breaths," not-Derrick says.

I do. I do a few box breaths and feel my heart rate slowing.

"Thanks."

"Let's just get out of here, man," he says. "We'll figure it all out from the road, okay?"

"Yeah, good idea," I agree, bending down and pulling him over to the waiting Jeep.

It takes a little effort, but I get him back in and close the gate before climbing in and starting it back up.

"I feel like I'm forgetting something," I say.

"The flashlight," he says from the back.

"Shit, you're right. My fingerprints are all over that thing, too. Good call."

"We make a good team," he says.

I can see the flashlight right where I left it, balanced on the rock, threatening to fall in.

"Be right back."

I jump out, run up to the hole, grab the flashlight, but before I turn to make my way back something stops me. I have the urge to look at her again. To see her face one more time.

I peek over the edge.

She looks so innocent. I can't imagine what would drive a person to hurt someone so beautiful.

"Who did this to you?" I ask, reaching down to touch her cheek. I pause before I do, thinking about the possibility of leaving DNA or something, but the hesitation is brief and I brush the hair from her forehead and tuck it behind her ear.

Back at the Jeep, not-Derrick is humming as I open the passenger-side door.

"Hey, buddy," he says, breaking his tune. "You think we could stop for grub? A burger or something?"

I set the woman on the passenger seat and buckle her in the best I can. Broken bones threaten to pop through the skin at the back of her neck as her head flops forward. I try a few times to get it to stay, but it falls to one side or the other every time.

I look in the back and see not-Derrick staring at me.

"You have got to be fucking kidding me, man," he says.

"I can't just leave her there. She looked so lonely," I try to explain, but as I say this, it both makes no sense and makes all the sense in the world.

"Seriously, dude, and I mean this with the full weight of the pun intended, but you're just digging your grave deeper and deeper."

I put my forearm on the headrest that the woman clearly isn't utilizing and lean in to ask, "*Is* that a pun?"

"Isn't it?"

"If you don't know, then I don't know either," I point out.

"Right."

I turn my attention back to the woman strapped into the front seat of my Jeep with her head threatening to fall off.

"I really think this is a bad idea," not-Derrick says again.

"I just need to find something to keep her head up," I say, looking around the Jeep, but I've taken almost everything out in preparation for transporting a dead body. I didn't prepare for two.

I open the glovebox and root around in there and a sigh of relief washes over me as I pull out the roll of electrical tape that every Jeep owner needs to have on hand.

"Perfect," I say.

I move back to the tailgate and pull it open.

"What are you doing?" not-Derrick asks.

I don't answer, I just move his legs and grab the tire iron that I used to crush his skull and stir his brains.

After a few minutes of trial and error, I manage to brace her head using the tire iron taped to the back of her neck, with the angled part keeping it from turning too far one way or the other. But in the low-cut black dress she wears, it looks a little strange with the black tape around her neck.

"Looks like shit," not-Derrick says.

"You think?" I ask, stepping back to see what it looks like from the outside.

"Yeah, looks like you taped a tire iron to a dead woman to hold up her fucking head so it doesn't fall off and rattle around on the floor."

"I've got it," I proclaim.

I unzip my hoodie and put it on her. With the hood up and the zipper all the way to the top, it's barely noticeable.

"Perfect," I say.

"Yeah, not bad," not-Derrick agrees.

"She looks kinda cute in my hoodie."

Not-Derrick does not agree with this, but I think it's just because he's jealous that she's up front with me and not lying cramped back there with him.

I climb behind the wheel and stare back out toward the main road.

"Okay, smart guy, what now?" not-Derrick asks.

I don't answer. I just drive. I've got a lot to figure out.

I get to the main road and start heading back down the mountain, thinking that maybe, if I get back toward an area I know a little better, something will come to me.

Getting lost in the small, stolen glances I take at the woman in the passenger seat next to me, I admittedly am not paying enough attention to the winding mountain roads, but I can't help it. She looks so peaceful. It's been a long time since I've had a woman riding with me.

I reach over and attempt to open her eyes, placing my fingers on her forehead and trying to pull up on the eyelid with my thumb. I get one open. They are light brown. Beautiful. Elegant.

"Look out!" not-Derrick shouts from the back, right as I catch something moving in the road in front of me out of the corner of my eye.

I tap the break and maneuver around the fox, but not-Derrick slams against the back of our seats, and the woman's head falls forward. A flaw in my taping system. It was fine unless some force pushed her head forward. I try to catch it so that it doesn't put too much strain on the skin holding it to the neck. I manage to slow down and navigate the Jeep off onto the gravel shoulder.

No way. The same spot I stopped earlier on the way up the road.

Once safely stopped, I'm able to get her head leaned back against the tire iron. Pulling the hood down over her brow and yanking the strings to tighten it seems to secure her head pretty well.

"That should do the trick," I say.

And then lights come around the curve. A fucking SUV. *The* fucking SUV.

"It can't be," not-Derrick says.

But it is. The old man veers toward me, cutting across the lane. I reach back and yank the tarp over not-Derrick just in time for the old man to pull up right next to me, his driver-side window right next to mine.

"Well, didn't think I'd see you still sitting here when I came back up this way," he says.

"Yeah, I think we're going to head back down tonight. Little too cold up there for my girlfriend," I say, nodding toward the woman in the passenger seat while also trying to block their view of her.

"Girlfriend?" not-Derrick says from under the tarp.

"Evening, ma'am," the old man says, trying to look around me.

I turn to look at her, hoping that the move will block her even more. She's staring at the dashboard with one eye open and the hood of my sweatshirt pulled so tight around her head that she looks like a cartoon character.

"She okay?" the younger man asks.

I whip my head back around and smile. "She's a bit of a drinker, had a bit too much wine for this altitude," I say, proud of a quick answer that sounds very plausible.

"Oh yeah, his mom was the same way, rest her soul," the old man says, and flashes the first truly friendly smile I've seen from him.

"Where are you all heading?" I ask, trying to shift the conversation back to them, and to remind them they were going somewhere when they stopped.

"We just went down the hill to have some supper, heading home now. We live just up there at the top of the mountain," he says, pointing into the darkness like I can see his place.

"Oh, wow. I bet that's nice," I say.

"There are worse places to call home for the summer," he says.

"I would guess so," I say, hoping that's the end of the pleasantries and he'll let me go.

"What're y'all doing on the side of the road?" the young man interrupts.

I hesitate.

"Navigation," not-Derrick says.

"Oh, navigation," I repeat. I reach down and pluck my phone from the cup holder. "Just putting in the best route home."

"Where you all from?" the old man asks. I know he wants to give me directions, but I really don't want him knowing where I live, just in case.

"Denver," I say. That's broad enough that it wouldn't help authorities even if it was true.

"I see," he leans out his window and points back down the mountain from where he came. "Just stay on this here road until you get to a fork in the road. Take the left, then stay on that until you get to I-70. Then head east. Got that?"

"Left at the fork, then I-70 East. Got it," I say.

When he turns back, he gets a glimpse of my passenger. He squints to get a better look.

"You sure she's okay?" he asks, poking a plump finger in her direction.

She's still just staring through her one open eye, but she looks cute doing it.

"Yeah, she's perfect. We just need to get her back home." To solidify this point I put the car in gear and let it roll a few inches.

"Well, take care of her," the old man says.

"Will do! You all have a good night. And thanks for the directions," I say, waving my hand out the window and pulling away from them.

I can see their suspicious looks in the rearview mirror as I drive away, throwing dust into the competing red glow of our taillights.

"Holy shit, that was close!" not-Derrick yells from the back.

"Right?" I say, reaching back and uncovering his face.

He takes a deep breath, as if it matters.

"Girlfriend, huh?" a beautiful voice asks from the passenger seat.

I have to fight to keep the car on the road. She's looking at me, both those browned-butter-colored eyes staring into my soul.

"Oh," I stutter, "I—I was just saying that to get us out of there."

"Well, it worked," she says. "Good job . . ."

"Oh, Eddie. Edward Lee Stewart, actually," I stammer out.

"I *knew* your name wasn't fucking Keegan," not-Derrick says.

"Edward Lee Stewart?" the woman says. "Sounds like some sort of serial killer."

"If the shoe fits," not-Derrick adds.

"Hey, shut up. 'Serial' means I've killed more than one person," I argue.

"I think it's cute," the woman says.

I can't help but smile as my face warms.

"Really?" I ask, soaking in the reassurance.

"Really?" not-Derrick repeats.

"Yeah, really," she says. The warmth in her voice tells me she means it.

"What's your name?" I ask.

"What do you think my name is?"

"Hmmm. Probably something cute," I say.

"Jesus Christ, man," not-Derrick says.

"What cute name?" she asks, both of us ignoring not-Derrick.

"I don't know, like Luna or Evie or something."

"Evie, that's it. You guessed it!" she squeals. "You're smart."

"Fucking kill me," not-Derrick says.

"You're already dead," I remind him.

"Kill me again."

"I would if I could," I joke.

"So, not that I'm not grateful," Evie starts, "but why did you pull me out of that hole? Why not just leave me there? I wasn't your problem. Now I am."

I'm not really sure how to answer that. She's cute, yeah, but she's also dead. I play with the heater a bit, fiddling with the knobs to kill time.

"I felt like it was the right thing to do," I finally say.

"Tampering with a crime scene was the right thing to do? Pretty sure there are laws about moving a corpse, too," not-Derrick says.

"I think it's sweet. Not many people would have done what you did. Especially for someone like me," Evie says.

"What's that mean? Someone like you?" I ask.

Right when I ask the question, though, I know what she's talking about. I suppose I knew before I asked. I knew when she said it. I made a snap judgment about her.

She doesn't respond.

"I'm sorry," I say.

The hum of the road carries us in relative silence for the next few minutes. I try to play it cool, but I want to look over at her and see if she's upset. I want to make it better. I glance over. She's just looking out the windshield, taking in what little bit can be seen in the Jeep's headlights.

"Psssst, hey," not-Derrick whispers.

I look over the seat at him.

"Hey," he says. "Does she look familiar to you?"

She does look a little familiar, but I can't place her.

"Is she an actress? Did we find a dead celebrity?" not-Derrick asks.

"Maybe," I say, worrying that I may have gotten myself into something more high profile than I am ready to deal with.

She's so pretty. She could be a model or an actress.

"You warm enough?" I ask.

"Yeah, I'm okay. Your hoodie is perfect. Smells nice, too. Thank you." Then she adds, "I appreciate you taking such good care of me."

That's all I've ever wanted to hear. That I was enough. I've only ever wanted a beautiful woman to tell me that I was enough.

"Thank you."

"For what, silly?" she asks.

"I don't know. I guess I just don't get a lot of recognition, you know? I work hard, try to be a good neighbor, I volunteer when I can."

"Murder pedophiles," not-Derrick adds. "Or try to, at least."

"You're such a noble person," Evie says before I can tell not-Derrick to shut up again.

"I've always tried to be, but no one has ever recognized it." I don't want to get too deep into my relationship with my parents with a woman I just met, so I leave it at that.

"Well, I do, and I appreciate it," she says.

My cheeks feel warm, but thankfully it's too dark to see that I'm blushing.

Not-Derrick must read the awkward silence, and he bails me out.

"Phew! Ex-*cuse* me! I'm sorry." He laughs. "You may want to crack a window."

It does smell like someone died in here, so I roll down the windows, letting the cool night air flow in.

"That's not too cold, is it?" I ask, looking over at Evie. She's got one little curl of hair that's snuck out from under her hood and it's blowing around in the breeze.

"No, it feels nice. Feels free," she says.

We drive for a few minutes with the quiet from the night filling the space like air in a balloon. I don't know what to say. The moment feels special. I glance over to see what Evie is doing, and she's looking at me. I smile. It's impossible not to. Her eyes fill my soul. It feels like we were meant to be. How is it that I am just now meeting her? She winks at me and my heart feels like it goes over a highway rumble strip.

I put eyes back on the road, watching the hood of the Jeep eat the earth in front of it. The moment is so close to perfect. So close to everything I ever wanted. There's just one thing missing.

I reach up and turn on the radio. It's quiet for a moment, and I have a pang of panic that a song just ended and we are about to be stuck with commercials. Or, even worse, we aren't getting a signal up here in the mountains. Then a song begins. I start to bob my head along with the beat. A few notes in and not-Derrick starts to sing. I laugh and shake my head.

"You're crazy," I call back to him over the music and the noise from the open window, but it just makes him sing louder.

Evie watches the trees roll by as she mouths the words to the song. She must feel me looking at her, but she just smiles. I take a chance.

"May I?"

She looks at me. Those eyes, windows to a soul I didn't know I was looking for.

She giggles. "What took you so long?"

I put my hand on her thigh, just beneath the hem of her skirt, above her knee, being respectful in the placement. Her skin is cool to the touch, so I rub in a small circle to try and warm her up.

"Sing with me," she says.

Fuck it. I start singing, too. We fly down the highway, through the mountains, belting out tunes and laughing. Rock songs, stadium anthems, a boy band song from when we were kids. We all seem to forget the same words to certain songs, but that doesn't stop us from selling our respective solos.

"Hey, man," not-Derrick says, interrupting my perfect rendition of "Free Fallin'." "Look."

We are passing the rest stop where he and I met. His car is still parked near the back where he left it. Part of me suspected there would be cops, that it would be a crime scene, but there's no one there.

"I wonder when they'll see all the blood," he says.

"It rained a little after," I reply, hoping that it would have helped a little, at least.

"How has no one noticed I'm gone?" he asks.

"I'm sure there are lots of people out looking for you, buddy," I say.

"You really think so?"

"For sure. I bet they just haven't made it this far up here yet."

"You're sweet," Evie says, giving me a smile and looking at me with those beautiful eyes. She makes me want to be the version of me that she sees.

"You know what?" I say, pulling the Jeep off the highway and into the rest area.

"What are we doing?" not-Derrick asks.

"I want to know my best friend's name," I tell him, pulling the Jeep in next to his car, putting my passenger-side door right next to his driver-side, just like I did the first time.

"Aw, come on, man. You're my best friend, too," he says. "Grab my phone, if you can find it."

Evie gives me another one of those looks that makes me feel like I can do no wrong, and I hop out of the Jeep.

There's no one there. This rest stop is off the beaten path, which was probably why the real Derrick picked it. The car door is unlocked, thankfully, and I pull my hand into my sleeve and use it to open it.

"Smart," not-Derrick yells. "Keep them prints off of things."

He'd left his keys, wallet, and phone in the car when he went to use the bathroom. The wallet is a bulky leather thing that has seen better days. I grab it, careful not to touch anything else. Still leaning in the car, I flip it open and check the driver's license.

"Tucker?!" I yell. "Whose name is *Tucker* anymore?"

"Oh, come on, man, it was my grandpa's name," he says. "I assume."

There's a phone in the cup holder and I grab it, too. As I do, the lockscreen turns on and I see a familiar face looking back at me.

"What the fuck?" I say, dropping into the driver seat.

Part Three: The Surprise

The lockscreen is a selfie of two women on a beach somewhere. They are smiling and happy. I turn to look into the window and see one of the women staring right back out at me.

"Evie?" I say.

There is another phone on a mount attached to the dashboard. I grab it and get out of the car, slamming the door hard when I do.

"Listen, man," not-Derrick—Tucker—says when I open the back of the Jeep. "I know what this looks like."

"Why do you have her phone, Tucker?" I hold it up to him.

"I don't know, man. I don't know how that got there."

I put her phone in my pocket and hold his up.

"What's the password?" I demand.

"I don't know."

I open the tarp and use his thumb to unlock it. I close the tailgate and get into the driver seat, forcing back tears.

"I'm sorry," Evie says.

"Just give me a minute, please?" I ask.

I go through Tucker's phone. I open his social media app and start scrolling.

"Hey, man, stop that. That's my personal stuff," he says.

"Fuck you. I thought we were friends. I thought I knew you."

"Knew me? You didn't even know my name."

Then I see it. A picture he posted with the caption, *Work Lunch*. The photo shows four other people, including a beautiful woman with short dark hair. Three of the people in the photo are tagged, and one of them is her. Her name is Jamie.

"Jamie?" I say. Not to her, but just to try it out in my mouth.

"I like Evie better," she says.

"Okay," I say, digging deeper into Tucker's phone.

I go to his friends list to see if the two of them are actually friends or if they just work together, and she isn't there. I scroll all the way through his eighty-four friends, and no sign of Jamie or Evie, but there is a name I recognize.

It's Clint. The friend I found the body spot with.

"Holy shit," Evie says.

I go to his messaging app to see if he had messaged Clint, and sure as shit, his most recent message is to him.

It's a map pin to the location of the body spot.

"You fucking asshole," I say.

"Come on, man," he says.

"Shut the fuck up, *Tucker*."

I scroll the messages and see one that makes my stomach turn.

Tuck Everlasting: hey

Jamie from Accounting: Hey?

Tuck Everlasting: its tucker from work

Jamie from Accounting: Tucker? How did you get my number?

Tuck Everlasting: I work in hr, remember? I've got access to everyone's number!

Jamie from Accounting: Oh, ok. Did you need something? I left the payroll charts in your box.

Tuck Everlasting: nothing boring like that. i wanted to see what you were up to tonight? want to get a drink?

Jamie from Accounting: That's very kind, thank you. But I'm already at the bus stop waiting to go home.

Tuck Everlasting: boring! come on, one drink.

Jamie from Accounting: I'm good, thank you though.

Tuck Everlasting: there you are

Jamie from Accounting: What?

Tuck Everlasting: let me give you a ride. its getting ready to rain

"You motherfucker," I yell over the seat at him.

"I'm sorry, man!" he cries.

"Fuck you, you piece of shit! You killed my girlfriend!"

"She wasn't your girlfriend at the time!"

I throw the Jeep in reverse and tear out of the parking lot, not knowing where I'm going, just that I don't want to be there.

"I'm sorry," Evie says. "I didn't want to go with him."

"I know, babe. I know," I say.

We ride in silence for a while before anyone speaks.

"I wish we had met sooner," Evie says.

"Me too," I reply. "I'm sorry I couldn't help you."

"You've done a lot."

I nod. "What are we going to do about him?"

"Don't start talking about me like I'm not fucking sitting right here," Tucker says.

"We should throw him off one of these mountains so it looks like an accident," Evie suggests.

"Jesus fucking Christ," he says. "You can't just go throwing people off fucking mountains."

"That's it," I say.

"What?" Evie asks.

"We'll go back to his car. There's a ridge right there, and I can throw him off head-first."

"To disguise the damage?" she asks.

"Exactly."

"Fuck you both," Tucker says.

I ignore him. "Then I'll leave both your phones unlocked and put them back in his car."

"That way, after they find his body, they find my phone," she says.

"And the text of where to hide your body," I say.

"That's smart," Evie says.

"It's fucking dumb. Come on, we're friends!" Tucker argues, and tries to sing a few words of one of the songs we sang, but we ignore him.

After a few minutes, we're back at the rest stop, and I am backed up to the ridge that drops off right behind it. I stare into the blackness below.

"You don't have to do this, bro," Tucker says from his spot on the tarp next to me.

"I think I do," I say.

"It won't make sense. There won't be enough blood. I lost too much already."

"I think the creek down there will help with that." I can't see the creek, but I can hear it. It's not deep enough, or powerful enough, to take his body, but it'll likely make the authorities think the blood just washed downriver.

I lift him up, peeling his sticky head off the tarp.

"Bro, come on, bro," he pleads.

"Stop calling me 'bro,' " I say, letting go of his body and allowing it to tumble forward so that his head smacks against a rock just a few feet below the ridgeline with a wet crack.

Then he is gone. Swallowed by the darkness. I hear him hit the side a few times, and then there is a wet slap as he lands in the creek among the rocks.

I roll up the tarp, careful not to get any of the blood on the ground, and put it back on the plastic in the Jeep. I wipe off the phones and return them to Tucker's car before getting back in the Jeep.

"I'm sorry about that," I tell Evie.

"Don't be. You're sweet," she says.

"I suppose we should drop you back off at the spot, huh?" I ask, not wanting to think about having to say goodbye.

"I guess so," she says, seemingly struggling with the same issue.

"What if we didn't?" I ask.

"Huh?"

"They'll already have the location and the conversation via text."

"I skinned my knee on the rocks when he shoved me down there, so there's skin, and I'm sure I left some hair or something there . . ."

"And if you had gone down the hole, they would have likely never been able to recover your body anyway," I finish her thought. "So your family will have closure."

"Exactly," she says with a smile.

"So what should we do instead?"

"Eddie?" she asks.

"Yes?"

"Would you do me a favor?"

"Of course. Anything."

"Bury my body somewhere nice."

"As you wish."

And tomorrow, I will.

ATOMIC

DESPAIR

R ain dribbled off the old, metal car-part man statue and onto the dry, cracked desert floor like blood onto busted lips. It had been ages since rain last dampened the dirt in the nothing little town that was once Piston Forge. The car-part man stood sentry at the road's edge in front of Albert's Food & Fuel Service Station. He was a well-built statue. His welds weren't perfect, but they were sturdy, and when your only job is to stand at the side of the road and greet the thousands upon thousands of automobiles that pass by on that particular tract of Route 66, strong is better than pretty, which was always what Albert would tell people his mother used to say to him when he was young, whenever anyone complimented the car-part man.

The car-part man's name was Hank. He hadn't had a name originally, but at some point in the early '40s some greasers carved *HUNK OF JUNK* into the metal base the car-part man stood on. Then they stole the oil can that had served as his head. When Albert discovered the vandalism the next morning he replaced the head with a chrome headlight from a 1940 Packard Super Eight One-Sixty Touring Sedan he'd found on the side of the road after a drag race gone wrong. There was something special about that headlight. Its installation was the moment when the car-part man gained consciousness. He couldn't *do* anything with it. He could only stand there, watch, and listen. So he did. He watched as Albert pulled his pocketknife out and changed the graffiti so it read *HANK OF JANK* instead. Albert said it made the car-part man sound regal, like a knight. Albert explained to guests that knights would stand guard at castle gates, so Hank was basically the protector of this realm, a job he took very seriously.

Hank had no concept of time, exactly, only a cursory knowledge of its passing. He watched from his place among the ever-intrusive brambles of silverleaf nightshade and spotted knapweed as the sun appeared in the sky from behind him every afternoon then disappeared over the horizon every evening. He wondered sometimes if the sun coming up in the morning behind him was as beautiful as it was when it set. He assumed so, thanks to the thousands of humans who had stood next to him, some posed exactly like him—arm raised, elbow bent, finger pointing, and thumb cocked—to take photos. They would often exclaim how beautiful the sun rising behind him was. He liked to think that he was the main attraction, but never having been afforded the ability to turn around and see the rising sun, he'd never know for sure.

If Hank could count he would know that it had been more than ten years since the service station saw its last visitor. He was aware that the road had been devoid of the travelers that once zipped by. Route 66 was no longer the emblem of American adventure. Nor was Piston Forge a place on the map where people would exit the highway to seek nostalgia. What Hank didn't know, or couldn't know, was that the tarmac that connected the road through Piston Forge to the main road had long since eroded, which meant that the only feasible way to get out to the old ghost town (if you could call a defunct service station and three-room motor lodge a town) was to go off-road, and with the state's removal of the sign that once pointed toward the rundown build-

ings, no one even knew the place existed.
Except of course Albert, who was the only
person Hank had seen in the last decade.

"I don't think they're ever coming back,"
Albert said one day, sitting at the peel-
ing picnic table that sat at the foot of the
eight-foot car-part statue. "The road's gone.
The people are gone. Nothing left out there.
Everyone's gone."

Hank stood, his chest, the repurposed gas
tank off a 1920 Indian Scout motorcycle,
raised high, as it had been for more than
sixty years. Rust had eaten away at him, bits
of him flaking off like small, oxidized pages
of a calendar counting down the days until he blew away in the wind. He'd accept-
ed his fate easily enough when the people
stopped coming. For a while after the cars
had stopped, Albert would crumple his frail
body into his faded pickup truck and rumble off, only to return hours later driving
erratically. Hank always wondered what was

happening behind him, as he could hear the breaking of bottles and cursing but could never see the conditions that led to the man's cries of despair. He only knew that the times when Albert would come sit at the table and talk to him were growing more and more infrequent. Hank's best friend was growing old.

"I'm eighty-eight years old, for God's sake," Albert said, looking up at Hank as if he could answer. Instead he just stood the way he had for all those decades, pointing out to the horizon.

Hank had spent decades listening to the people sitting at the picnic tables as they came and went. The children would run around playing tag, thankful to have reprieve from the backseats of their parents' station wagons. They'd eat the "big three P moneymakers," as Albert would call them: popcorn, pretzels, and popsicles. The parents always sat and talked while drinking coffee, soda pop, or beer, and smoking endless cigarettes, the butts of which would often be flicked up at Hank. The people at the tables would go through phases of what was important news for the day. For a while, early on, they would come and talk about the war of the world. Then they were afraid of "the bomb." They'd talk about how at any minute they could all be turned into ash. Then things changed. People were happier, for a while. They would come in little buses with flowers in their hair and talk about "free love" while they smoked something they called pot. (Those butts weren't flicked at him though.) Then, everyone seemed to be afraid again. They claimed the Russians had "the bomb." Or the Cubans. It was all very hard to follow, and Albert always seemed scared.

Then the people stopped coming. The cars no longer sped by on the road that Hank overlooked. Over the years the wind had blown dirt across the pavement and the road was consumed by the desert. Hank hoped that one day it would be cleared and the people would come back. Instead the only tracks in the dirt were Albert's—until those stopped too.

"I think the world is over, buddy. I think it's moved on," Albert said, his knees and back popping as he stood up from the picnic table. If Hank could have helped he would have. It pained him to see Albert, his only friend, his creator, struggling to stand. Albert stumbled back to the lodge and out of Hank's view.

It would be a few sunsets, Hank didn't know how many, before the rain day. The day he would see Albert for the last time.

"Well—" Albert said before a coughing fit stopped him. He leaned on the table, trying to hold himself up while his body convulsed. Blood dripped out between his dry lips and he spit it into the dirt that was starting to soak up the rain.

When the coughing stopped, Albert stood as straight as he could and brushed himself off. His old coveralls hadn't been cleaned in years, so it didn't really change anything. Albert turned and looked out over the desert. The clouds were dark, pregnant with rain.

Albert gazed back at Hank, tears welling like the clouds above him. He reached his gnarled hand up and grabbed Hank's arm, pulling himself to his gas-tank chest and squeezing him.

"If I had to see the end with someone, I'm glad it was with you, my friend," he said. He rapped a knuckle on the tank, giving it a hollow *thong*, and stepped back down into the dirt.

When Albert turned and started walking, Hank knew exactly where he was going.

He didn't know much about death except what Albert had told him. Sometime after the people had stopped coming along, Albert's dog, Sandy, had passed away. Albert had loved that dog so much. He'd sit at the picnic table and toss a ball out into the desert and Sandy would run out, kicking up a mess of dust, grab it, and bring it back, every time. It was the happiest Hank had ever seen his friend. So when poor Sandy died, he watched as Albert wrapped her in a blanket, carried her out into the desert where she used to run, and buried her so that Hank could watch over the little cross Albert had stuck in the ground. A knight doing his duty.

After Sandy was gone, Albert said he had nothing left to live for. That the world had ended and there was nothing left.

Hank watched as Albert stumbled through the forming mud, leaving footprints that led all the way out to where the cross stood out in the desert. It didn't look like he was going to make it, but there wasn't much that could stop Albert when he set his mind to something. When he finally made it, he balanced himself with the cross as he lowered onto his knees. His head dipped to his chest, and he sat that way, soaking in the rain, for a long time. Too long, Hank thought, until his only friend fell sideways onto the grave of the only thing that meant as much to Albert as Albert meant to Hank.

Countless sunsets passed. Hank never stopped watching over his friend or his dog. He watched as the man got smaller and smaller. He watched, wanting to call out, as small things fed on him. Thankfully he was far enough away that he couldn't watch with much clarity, but it was obvious enough what was happening.

Hank supposed this was a good thing. From what he figured the world had moved on, like Albert had said. He'd heard people talking about "the bomb" enough that it seemed obvious what had happened. Someone had finally used it. They'd blown up all the people, and the ones who didn't blow up got radiation poison, which one man, claiming to be a scientist, once told Albert was worse than getting vaporized by the blast. Was that what happened to Albert? Had the radiation finally got him? Had he been the last one left? With how strong he was, it was the only logical explanation. It made sense that Albert survived the bomb, and whatever great wars that followed.

But he was gone now. Just a pile of sticks and rags out in the desert.

Hank couldn't remember where he was before Albert had given him the headlight the morning he began to think. He suspected that wherever it was, that was where Albert and Sandy were now, and he wanted nothing more than to be there too.

Days passed like sand through an endless hourglass. There was nothing but the setting sun to anchor Hank in time. Days were spent trying to recall all the people who had passed through Albert's Food & Fuel Service Station. All the people he had protected as a knight throughout the years. He could remember a surprisingly large number of them. He supposed when you couldn't do anything but watch and listen you got good at doing both, and by that time (though he didn't know this) he had been doing it for almost a century.

Albert's footprints lasted for a long time, tracks left like some prehistoric creature had pressed them into the earth. Eventually the wind covered them, and Hank watched as they slowly disappeared back into the desert, gone forever.

Then, one day while he was watching small wisps of clouds float by, something broke the normal quiet sound of the wind across the desert. A bark echoed across the barren land. Sandy? No, it wasn't Sandy. It was a dog that was about the same size but which looked different. Sandy had long fur the color of sand—hence her name—and floppy ears that bounced when she ran. This dog was taller, leaner, and had short black fur with some white spots and ears that pointed up like little antennae. If Hank had a heart, it would have swelled. The dog was the most exciting thing he had seen in a very, very long time, and something he never thought he would see again.

But it wasn't the most exciting thing he would see that day.

The dog had come over the far hill where the road used to lead. It would run a few feet, stop, spin around, look back, and then continue running toward Hank. Before the dog made it halfway to Hank there was another sound. This time it was a whistle. The dog stopped to look back.

It wasn't alone.

Hank waited, wanting whatever it was to come up over the hill so he could finally see what still roamed the wastelands that he was sure the world had been reduced to. Somehow someone had survived the blast and the radiation.

The person who followed the dog over the hill was covered in rags, wrapped up like it was cold, though the sun was beating down. As the figure drew closer it was clear that the wrap around their head was thin, used to block the sun rather than cold. Portable shade—the survivors of the bomb were adapting. Perhaps they were more sensitive to the sun now. Or, worse, perhaps their skin had been burned off. Hank almost didn't want to see if that was the case, but watched intently as they crossed the dusty expanse.

"Ratchet!" the person called from under the wrap. The dog looked up toward Hank, then turned and ran back toward its companion. "Good boy." The person scratched behind the dog's ears as he jumped up at the shielded figure. "Well, look at this," the person said, slinging a heavy backpack onto the picnic table in front of Hank. "Looks empty."

Of course it was empty. What else would it be? The world had ended. As excited as Hank was, the knight in him was coming out. This was the first person who had ever been to Albert's Food & Fuel Service Station without Albert being there as well.

It was a woman. Of course it was. Women had always seemed more resilient to Hank. She removed the wrap around her head and shook the sand that had managed to blow under it out of her ponytail.

After dusting herself off the woman pulled a water bottle from her backpack and took a drink before putting a small dish on the ground and pouring some water into it for Ratchet. She looked around while the dog lapped at the water in the dish.

"Hmmm," she pondered, then pulled something from her pocket. It was a flat plate of some kind. A black rectangle the size of her hand.

Magic happened next. The black rectangle lit up and colors richer than Hank had seen in decades flashed across the front of it. That was it. That's how this woman had survived. She was a witch. She carried magic in her pocket.

"No service," she said, before ending the spell that brought the magic colors to her device.

No, Hank thought, there hadn't been service there since the mid-seventies or so, when the gas trucks stopped coming.

The woman wore torn jeans and a T-shirt with a man that seemed to be holding a sword made of pure light on it, standing with a woman holding onto his leg. Perhaps it was a creed or representation of whatever roving band of refugees she belonged to.

"Are you the proprietor of this establishment . . ." She looked down at the base where his name was scratched. ". . . Hank of Jank?"

Hank wanted to tell her that he was not, that he was merely the guard, and that the owner, *the* Albert of Albert's Food & Fuel Service Station, lay just a few hundred feet behind her, hidden by the bramble, but of course he could not.

"Well, Hank of Jank, I'm Jillian of the Salt Lake, but you can call me Jillian," she said, turning to pull something from her bag but then whipping back around to point at Hank. "Never Jill. Jillian. Got it?" She looked at him for a moment. "Good."

Were there metal post-apocalyptic beings that *could* talk? Did she think he was one of them? Hank was unsure, but he certainly hoped this woman—Jillian, never Jill—would tell him of the world, even if he couldn't respond.

"We might crash here for a night or two, if you don't mind?" she asked.

Hank still couldn't respond, but if he could he would welcome her. He thought that Albert might have also.

"Shit! Not my *Star Wars* shirt," Jillian exclaimed. She tried scraping the jelly from the front of her shirt that had slurped out from the sandwich she was trying to press into her mouth.

Star Wars. The world war had moved beyond the planet and made it to the stars! People had come before and talked about something called Sputnik, and claimed the

"Russkies" were going to use satellites to destroy everyone. It sounded like maybe they finally had.

Jillian jumped up onto the platform with Hank and got a closer look. Hank liked having someone so close. He had forgotten how young people could look, how spry they could be.

"You've seen better days, my friend." Jillian pulled a small flake of rust from his side. "I think if I'm going to be here for a while we should take care of that."

And she did. Jillian stayed. Not just for a few days, but for weeks. Or maybe it was months. It was hard to tell. Having someone with so much energy stay there gave him things to watch. Between Ratchet running around and Jillian doing all sorts of other things he was never bored. The second day she was there she got Albert's old pickup running and she loaded Ratchet in and drove away. Hank had worried at first that they wouldn't come back, but they did.

Then, just as she promised, Jillian started working on Hank. The sanding tickled a little, but it wasn't like he could laugh or anything, and after a while it just felt really nice. One day she brought cans of chrome spray paint and gave him a complete makeover.

"You're going to be brighter than the sun, you beautiful, shiny man!" When she said that she jumped up onto the platform, pulled herself up, and kissed his head, the only truly chrome part of his body.

She jumped down and looked around at the place. She'd fixed the motel up a little as well, though Hank couldn't see that. He was just taking her word for it.

They found Albert. One morning Ratchet ran out too far and came back with something in his mouth. Jillian seemed scared, and she went out to where the cross was. When she got back she told Hank she saw that it was someone's dog out there, and that she assumed it was the person who was lying beside it. She said it wasn't right, so she'd dug a hole next to the dog's grave and put its owner in so he would be safe next to her.

Jillian liked to talk, a lot more than Albert ever had. She said talking to Hank was like "free therapy." He didn't know what that meant, but it seemed to help her, so he was very glad to listen. She would talk about her parents and how terrible they were. She talked about being an artist and wanting to travel the world making art. The more she told him the more Hank started to think that the world wasn't as poorly off as they had thought. He wished Albert was still around to hear that.

Jillian had been planning to buy a van, build it out, and then live in it, driving around the country putting her art on something called the inter-net. She'd "borrowed" some money from a guy she was dating, without telling him, to buy the van, but apparently the money didn't belong to her boyfriend. It belonged to some "dickhead" who sold drugs. That term made Hank concerned that maybe, in fact, there *were* mutations due to radiation, but Jillian did not expound on that. She just said that if they found her they would kill her. They took the van she'd bought, so she hightailed it out of town and had been looking for a way to escape when she found Albert's.

Since it was so far outside of town, and there wasn't a way to get there without knowing where it was and driving off-road, she felt pretty safe there. She was handy and had fixed the truck, so she was able to go to the nearest little town and get supplies, at least until her money ran out. Which it was, and quickly. Hank hoped she would find a way to get more money. He wanted her to stay. He really liked Jillian. She was fun and entertaining, and she treated him like a person, even though he had nothing to offer her in return. He just stood looking out over the desert, pointing at nothing.

Then came another rain day.

Jillian had left early in the morning, when there wasn't a single cloud in the sky. By the time the sun had got to where Hank could see it, the clouds were full, and dark, and angry.

It rained a little. The water just beaded and ran off of Hank, with his fancy new paint job, but the thirsty desert soaked up as much water as it could. It wasn't enough to settle the dust, however, as a cloud of it rose up just over the hill, coming from the direction where the main road used to be, and it was accompanied by the unmistakable roar of Albert's truck.

The truck crested the hill and tore down the near side, throwing a plume of grit and rock into the air. As the truck flew by, Hank could see Jillian in the cab, and she looked panicked. She slammed on the brake and skidded to a stop somewhere behind him, jumping out and running somewhere.

"How in the fuck did he find me?" she yelled. "No, Ratchet, you stay in the truck!"

Things were slammed around, and then the truck door closed again. But then there was someone else—a vehicle coming over the hill, plowing through the still-settling dust that had been thrown up by the truck.

It was a van, but it didn't look like the ones Hank was accustomed to seeing. The door on the side was dirty and white and did not match the worn blue of the rest of the vehicle. The only consistency the van seemed to have was that all of its parts were dirty and rusty. The driver, who Hank could just barely make out as they sped by, appeared to be a mutation of some sort. Their hair was completely gone from one side of their head, and the hair growing from the top was a green shade the likes of which he had never seen.

The vehicle slid to a stop behind him, and it sounded as if multiple people were getting out.

"Where do you think you're going?" a deep voice asked.

"Get the fuck out of the way, Parker. I'll run your ass over," Jillian cried.

She sounded so scared. Hank wanted to break loose and help her, or at least see what was happening. She wasn't alone, though. Ratchet started barking the sort of bark only a good dog protecting its human can.

"Get out of the truck, and leave that fucking dog in there," the voice that was likely Parker said.

"Fuck you!" Jillian said. "Oh, what? Are you going to fucking shoot me?"

"Get out of the truck, Jill," he said.

She doesn't like being called Jill, Hank thought.

"Don't call me that, you fucking dick-head," Jillian said.

The truck door opened and then closed. Ratchet barked from inside.

"Tie her up and put her somewhere safe until we figure out what's what," Parker told someone.

"Don't you fucking touch me," Jillian yelled.

There was what sounded like a small scuffle, then a slap.

"Listen to me," Parker said. "You've caused a lot of fucking problems, and now I've got some real shitty people up my ass. So I need you to sit down and shut the fuck up while we work this out."

"And what does 'working it out' look like?" Jillian asked.

"Well, that depends. We have to see what *he* says."

"You have the van. Just take it," Jillian begged.

"And what about the rest of it? You use it to buy this truck?" Parker asked.

"Take it. Take the truck. You'll have the van and the truck. That's got to be worth what I took."

"Well, we'll find out what he wants us to do. Then you'll either go on your merry way, or I'll put a fucking bullet in your brain."

"Fuck you," Jillian yelled, but her voice sounded like she was running.

"Want me to get her?" another man's voice asked.

Then Jillian was in Hank's sight. She was running, but she stopped when Parker yelled after her.

"Stop, or I'll shoot your precious fucking dog!"

She stopped but didn't turn.

"Come back," Parker said.

Jillian did.

"Tie her up and put her in one of these rooms," Parker said. "Doesn't look like we are getting any signal, so one of you needs to take the van and go relay the message."

"I'll go," a third man's voice said. "I don't have much taste for this kind of thing anyway."

After a moment the van backed out and was leaving, puffing the dirt up once again. It was impossible to hear what was happening behind him as the van drove away on the gravel drive. Once it was gone, he could hear them talking, but it didn't sound like Jillian was among them.

"This place is rad," a woman's voice—not Jillian's—said.

"Yeah, I bet no one even knows this place exists anymore," another man's voice said.

"Is there electricity? What about water?" the woman asked.

"What's the matter, Nichi? You can't go a few minutes without a shower?" Parker replied.

"No, Parker, I am perfectly fine not showering. I just wanna know if I'll be able to shit without having to worry about a gecko climbing up my snatch. Is that too much to ask?" Nichi shouted back.

Wood splintered and snapped as one of them kicked in a door. From the sound, it was most likely one of the motel rooms.

"It's pretty dirty in here, but it's not a bad spot."

"Looks like she only fixed up the one room."

"That's good," Parker replied. "Means she's probably out here alone."

"Brad, what about the bathroom?" Nichi yelled, presumably to the man kicking in doors.

"The toilets work!" Brad called out, following a distant flush. "Must be on a well with a septic system."

"Can't believe it still works."

Brad was correct. Albert had the septic installed during the building of the motel. Before that he had slept in a storage closet inside the service center, and he and the visitors to the property had to use an outhouse.

"Hey," Parker called to the others. His voice sounded like he was directly behind Hank. "Look at this fucking thing."

The man stepped around into view. He wore a black jacket, the kind the bad boys on motorcycles used to wear when they would come through and harass Albert. Except his was adorned with patches. Iconography that Hank didn't recognize, mostly. Though there was one that he recalled was referred to as a swastika, thanks to a group of bikers who rode through and started some trouble once. The man in the jacket was drinking from a glass bottle, something folks that would come by Albert's would often buy. The clear bottles were soda, but the brown bottles were always beer. This bottle was brown.

"What is it?" Nichi called.

"It's one of those car-part statues. The ones that were popular back in the fifties and sixties, I think."

The man tipped the bottle back, dumping the rest of the liquid down his throat, then cocked his arm and threw the bottle at Hank. Glass exploded like a firework as the bottle connected with the side of Hank's head. Rancid liquid dripped down his headlight.

This wasn't the first time someone had hit him with something. Occasionally a child had thrown a rock at him, hoping to hit

him in the chest and hear the loud *THONG!*
sound that it made. It would leave a few
scratches and dents, but the way the children laughed always made it worth it. This
group was laughing, but it certainly did not
make it better. If the children's throwing
ever got out of hand Albert would come out
and scold the person doing it. There was a
hollow pang of sorrow as he was reminded
of his friend and how much he had cared for
Hank.

Another bottle smashed against the back
of Hank's head, followed by a trill of laughter.

"Hey, check this out," Brad said, having
yet to come around into Hank's view.

There was a sound, like a ball bearing in a
tin can, then a *pssssssst*. Hank felt something
cold go across his lower back.

He knew what this was. It was spray paint.
But likely not the beautiful chrome that Jillian had used. He wanted to move, but he

couldn't. Albert had built him and put him there to watch the road. He couldn't give up his post.

Parker looked up at Hank, who was nearly two full feet taller than him.

"Look at this piece of shit," he said. "I bet Jillian did this."

He ran his finger across the chrome paint on Hank's chest.

"You think she built it?" Brad asked.

"Nah, I think she just painted it. Seems like something she would do," Parker replied.

"How old do you think it is?" Brad asked.

"Probably forty or fifty years," Nichi replied as she strode up next to Parker and dropped a tattooed arm across his shoulders.

The two of them stepped back, smirking at something that Hank couldn't see. Though as soon as he felt the warm liquid splashing against the drive shaft he used for a left leg, he knew what it was. The other man, Brad, was peeing on him.

"Put that tiny little dick away and let's figure out what other treasures our new hideout holds while we wait for Hern to get back," Parker said. He took Nichi's hand from his shoulder and twirled her around, then led her back toward the station.

"Biggest one *you've* ever seen," Brad said, spraying a few squirts onto Hank's foot.

"Whoa, what the fuck are you doin'?" Parker yelled from what sounded like the lodge.

"What is it?" Brad called after them.

"Jillian's over here trying to escape. I thought you tied her up?" Parker yelled back.

"Want me to shoot her in the leg?" Nichi asked.

"Fuck all of you!" Jillian yelled.

There was a smacking sound and Jillian screamed.

Hank could feel something inside of himself starting to churn.

A cloud of dust signaled the return of the van and the one they called Hern. He pulled in and stopped just out of Hank's view.

"Keep her here. If she moves, stab her in the leg," Parker said. "Hern! That was quick. What did he say?"

"I just needed to drive a mile or so out to the highway and I got signal. So I called him," Hern said.

"And?"

"He said he didn't need her and there was no point in keeping her around. He did say, however, that he was very interested in this place. So he said do what we want with the bitch, then sit tight and he'll be out here first thing in the morning to check it out."

"Well," Parker said, "guess we better do this soon and hunker down. I think it's about to piss rain."

There was silence for a moment. Hank tried to listen for Jillian, but there was nothing.

"All right," Parker finally said. "Let's go take care of her."

The footsteps across the gravel drive felt more like the ticks of a time bomb as they got farther from Hank and closer to Jillian.

"What did he say?" Nichi asked.

Parker didn't answer, at least not so that Hank could hear it, but maybe he had signaled something.

"Hey, no, stop!" Jillian cried. "You don't need to do any of this. I'll fucking leave. I'll just take the dog and I'll go! You'll never see me again. You can tell him I'm dead. I'll let you take pictures to make it look like it. Come on, babe . . . you don't need to do any of this."

Jillian's voice was drowned out by the sound of Ratchet barking in the cab of the truck. Then there was a gunshot—a sound

Hank knew well, as people loved shooting at old cans out behind the motel. Glass broke somewhere, and Ratchet stopped barking.

Laughter cackled across the desert floor, muffling something else. A sound hidden in noise. It was Jillian. She moaned. It was a painful sound, one that Hank seemed to be able to key in on. He'd been listening to Jillian's voice for a long time now. He would know it anywhere. So when she cried out, the words shook him to his rivets.

"Someone, help me, please!"

A bark, again, from the cab of the truck.

"Tell your fucking dog to shut up, Jillian! The last one was a warning, the next one goes in its fucking brain!" Parker yelled.

"No! Stop!" Jillian pleaded. "Ratchet, it's okay . . . I'm okay, sweetie. Don't worry."

This seemed to work, as the barking stopped again.

"Hey!" Brad yelled.

"Stop her!" Parker followed.

"Bitch!" Nichi yelled.

There was the sound of a scuffle, and Jillian cried out again, her pain resonating through the air.

"Fuuuuuck!" Jillian yelled.

"You want another one? Fucking try and run again and I'll shove this knife so far into your fucking—"

There was a solid *thunk* and it was Parker's turn to yell in pain.

"Did you just headbutt me, you bitch?"

The shrill cry that followed did something to Hank. It . . . hurt. He *felt* it. Actually felt it. And then he heard the most painful two words he'd heard in the eighty years he'd been conscious.

"Hank, help!" Jillian cried.

Something snapped. First mentally, in the man made of discarded auto parts, and then something physical. Rust from generations of stale desert air popped between bolts and washers as metal began to move. Hank did something he had never done before.

He turned his head and looked back toward the lodge.

Jillian lay in the dirt, blood seeping from wounds in both legs, one just above the knee and the other higher up on her thigh. Parker sat on his knees next to her, blood dripping from his nose, holding a large knife. The others just stood around and watched, but the one they called Hern held a gun. Jillian tried to crawl but just fell face-first into the arid dirt.

Brad knotted his fingers into Jillian's hair. He yanked up hard and the hair peeled from the woman's scalp like velcro. Jillian let out a scream of pain and fell back into the dust.

"Ha! Look at that?" Brad said, holding the hair out, first to Parker and then Nichi, who seemed entertained.

Hank pulled at the lag bolts that held his feet flat against the steel plate he'd called home all those years. He wanted to go to Jillian, wanted to save her from the pain, but he was stuck.

"Let's try that again," Brad said, dropping the hair and wrapping his hand in its black leather glove around Jillian's neck, pulling her to her feet. She struggled to stand, but Brad squeezed her neck and held her there.

Jillian scratched weakly at his hand. Her face began to change, something Hank had seen once before when a boy with a silly cap fell backward from the table while eating one of the three Ps—a pretzel. It became lodged in the boy's throat and after a few moments his face was the same shade that Jillian's was now.

"What are you gonna do now?" Brad asked. "Hey, wake up."

Brad tried to push Jillian's eyelids open. Jillian could only respond by drooling and rolling her eyes back into her head. It was the same thing the pretzel boy had done before his father managed to dislodge the bread and get him breathing again. Hank wished with every bolt in his body that they would let Jillian breathe the same way.

"Let her go," Parker said, tapping Brad on the shoulder.

Brad let her go immediately, dropping the unconscious woman to the ground again.

"He said wake up," Nichi said, delivering a kick to Jillian's side.

Jillian stirred and put her arms over the ribs that the kick had likely broken.

"Aw, what's wrong?" Nichi asked.

The woman straddled Jillian's chest and dropped down. Jillian's ribs snapped like dry branches in a burning forest. Nichi sat atop her while she tried to scream, but only gasps in the way of prayers came out.

"I think that one really got her, Nichi," Parker said. "She doesn't look too happy."

"No?" Nichi asked. She leaned closer to Jillian and dug both thumbs into her mouth, forcing it into a grin. Jillian's teeth, previously a brilliant white, were now slick with blood.

"Stand her up," Parker demanded.

Nichi stood, grabbing Jillian by the shirt and pulling her back up.

Brad hooked his arms under Jillian's, then wrapped them around to cup both hands behind her neck and yanked her to her feet. Nichi grabbed a handful of Jillian's remaining hair and tried to hold her head up, but as soon as she let go it dropped back down, cracking her teeth together as her chin bounced off her chest.

A flash of lightning ripped across the sky as Hank pulled hard against the bolts in his feet, straining against them, pulling so hard that it felt like his knee and hip may snap first. His arm—the one that had spent the better part of a century pointing out over the road in front of him—creaked and moved, then fell and banged off his side, but the noise was masked by a kick drum of thunder that shook the few windows left in the motel and service station. Hank used his now free hand to pull up on his leg, trying everything he could to break loose.

The lightning had unzipped the sky, and the heavens began pouring down on the long-forgotten rest stop. What began as a light rain quickly became a storm, matched in its power only by the rage growing in Hank. Had he brought this on? Had he summoned the storm? Was that even something he could do? Up until that point he hadn't been able to move, so all things were possible.

"Fuck, man, we can't be hanging out out here! We're gonna get struck by lightning or some shit," Brad yelled from his place behind Jillian.

"Just hold her for a second," Parker called back over the sound of the beating rain.

Parker lifted the blade. It was huge and had a serrated edge that looked like teeth ready and willing to chew through whatever they were fed.

"Do it," Brad yelled.

"Go on, baby! Do it," Nichi agreed.

"Go!" Hern said.

Parker plunged the knife through the soaked shirt Jillian wore and into the soft skin of her belly. She woke, her head flying up as she screamed. Rain beat off of her face but didn't stop the wails. Parker jerked the knife upward, sending blood and bits of Jillian into the mud around her feet. He pulled the knife back, opening the floodgates to allow everything that was Jillian to be expressed in a wave of red.

Hank tried to mimic the wail that Jillian had let out, but he had no way to do so, so instead he stretched his hand out toward his last friend. A tingle went through him and electricity cracked in his joints.

A bolt of lightning reached down from the black molasses that was the clouds above, streaking over the motel and the group of marauders, and grabbed Hank's outstretched hand.

"Shit!" Parker yelled.

"We gotta get inside!" Nichi screamed as she ran for the door they had kicked in.

The others followed, slamming the broken door as the last one went through.

Something had changed inside Hank. The lightning had made him something more than he was before. He held his hands up in front of the headlight that was his face and flexed his fingers. They weren't difficult to move. He looked down at his feet, still bolted to the stand, then lifted them, popping the lag bolts like the candy sticks the kids used to dip in sugar.

Hank stepped down off his perch, finding his balance on his newly usable legs before hobbling as quickly as he could to where Jillian lay.

She was on her back, her intestines run out and sagging between her spread legs. Hank knelt next to her and, to his surprise, she turned her head to look at him. The life in her eyes was fading quickly. Hank slid his hand under his friend's head and lifted it up to hold her against the gas-tank chest she had painted, to protect her face from the rain in her dying moments.

Jillian raised one bloody hand, resting it against Hank's head. As her life left her, her hand slid down, leaving a smear of blood across the thick glass of the headlight. The blood was washed off by the heavy rain almost immediately, but Jillian wasn't alive to see it.

Hank didn't know if sorrow was what he was feeling. He didn't actually know if *feeling* was a thing he could do. Whatever was happening inside of him was big. It felt like he could explode like the fireworks Albert would light off a few times a year back when all the people were still alive.

Jillian seemed weightless as he lifted her and carried her through the storm, intestines dragging in the mud behind him, dipping into the divots the heavy metal man left as they went.

He took her to the truck, opened the door, and set her inside with Ratchet, who gave Hank a very confused look before taking to licking Jillian's face, his futile attempt to try and wake her.

Hank pushed the door to the cab closed just as the door to the motel opened. He wasn't sure what his plan was. He'd never had to *make* a plan before.

"How the fuck did I get volunteered for this shit?" Hern yelled back into the room.

The rain was coming down in sheets and the visibility was low, so the man in the doorway didn't seem to notice the eight-foot-tall robot standing on the other side of the parking area behind the pickup.

"Just get the beer and get back in here, you fuck! You're letting the rain in," Parker called from inside the room.

Hern pulled the door shut and took off in a sprint across the now muddy drive toward the van. He had his jacket pulled up in an attempt to shield himself from the rain. This gave Hank an advantage.

Hern reached the van and jerked the side door open and leaned in. He slid a large blue cooler across the van floor and attempted to lift it.

"Fuck, why did they think this was light enough for one person?" he said, flipping the top up and revealing that it was packed with ice and bottles of beer.

Moments later there was a knock at the motel door.

"Your fucking hands too full?" Brad yelled from inside before opening the door.

Hank stood cloaked in the darkness of the storm, just outside of view.

"What the fuck?" Brad said, looking down at the cooler that sat in the rain outside the door.

"What is it?" Nichi said, pushing past Brad and seeing the cooler. "Well, at least he brought the beer!"

Nichi flipped the lid of the cooler open, no doubt in hopes of finding a cold, refreshing beverage, but instead found 195 pounds of Brad, ripped to pieces and shoved with the force of a hydraulic suspension into a forty-eight-quart Coleman. Hank had taken the liberty to make sure the man's face was laid out nicely across the top, just to make sure they weren't confused as to who it was.

Nichi screamed, covering her mouth and falling against the doorframe. Brad saw it and froze. Parker, who seemed to be the most capable of them all, ran up to see what the commotion was. His expression was Hank's favorite. Parker's face was plastered with confusion rather than horror.

"What the fuck?" Parker asked in an almost conversational tone. Then, as if realization had struck, he looked over to where they had left Jillian to see that she was gone. "How?"

The sky lit up, not from lightning, but from Hank. The light shone from his face, blinding the three and driving them back into the room. They clambered inside, slamming the door behind them.

"Who's out there?" Parker called through the door. "Jillian? Jillian, I will fucking shoot you in the fucking face!"

Hank turned off the light, walked up, flipped the lid to the cooler closed, and snapped both latches tight. He lifted it by one handle, spun at the waist, and launched it through the front window of the room where the remaining three murderers hid.

The cooler shattered the old plate glass like it wasn't even there and shot across the room, smashing into the back wall, where it exploded, splattering all that was Hern all over the room.

"Jesus Christ!" someone screamed from inside the room. "Hold the door!"

It sounded like Parker. Still trying to give orders.

Hank opened his metal hands and shot them in on either side of the doorjamb, ripping the entire frame out of the building and leaving the three of them cowering, covered in Hern.

"Fuck me!" Brad yelled.

Parker attempted to run past the large metal man, but Hank was too fast. He leaned forward, shoving the man against the wall with the tie-rod he used as a forearm.

"Get the fuck off me!" Parker yelled.

But Hank remembered what this man had done. He remembered everything. He raised his large metal hand, placing it directly between himself and Parker's face so they could choose together. He looked at his fingers. The one he used to point was on this hand. It was a series of lug nuts welded together. Another was a few pistons, cut and welded together. He flexed these in Parker's face before getting to the third finger, which was not a car part at all, but the business end of a giant flat-head screwdriver. Hank held it up to Parker's face and nodded. Then he jammed it into his left thigh.

Jean and skin popped as the chisel tip dug into the meat of his thigh. He screamed and tried to drop to the ground, but Hank held him against the wall.

"Let him go, fucker!" Brad yelled, pointing a gun at Hank.

Hank looked at Brad. The barrel of the gun was less than a foot from the glass of his headlight. Without breaking his gaze, Hank slowly pulled the screwdriver from Parker's thigh.

"Now let him go," Brad demanded.

With the same methodical, slow speed at which he had pulled the screwdriver from Parker's left thigh, he pressed it into the man's right knee. The sound of breaking bone was only silenced when Brad pulled the trigger.

To Hank, the shattering of the headlight was louder than the bang from the small-caliber pistol. Glass rained down on Parker as Hank let go of him and slammed his hand down onto Brad's head.

"Stop!" Brad screamed, and fired multiple shots into Hank's chest. Small holes popped into the chrome and left exit wounds in his back.

Hank closed his metallic hand over Brad's head, pulling hair and skin with it. Hank lifted the man, but his scalp only held for a moment before it tore free from his skull and the man dropped. But Hank was fast. He shot out his other hand, still dripping with Parker's blood and bits of bone and ligament, and caught Brad around the neck. He lifted him, adding pressure, and watched the man's face go red, waiting for the color that matched Jillian's when the man had done this same thing to her.

Brad's face never reached that particular shade of purple, however, as the anger pushed Hank, and he squeezed a little too hard, a little too fast. Brad's head, which was already covered in blood from the lack of any skin above his eyebrows, popped off.

Nichi jumped out the window and ran across the muddy drive toward the van, but Hank wasn't done. He felt like it wouldn't be fair to let her go.

She made it to the van, and even managed to get herself into the driver's seat, but there were no keys. Hern had them. Hank knew this because he remembered, as he had pressed the man into paste, feeling them being ground into what had been Hern's pelvis. Unless someone had a spare, that van wasn't going anywhere.

Hank opened the door and stood looking in at Nichi.

"Just fuck off, man! What the fuck?"

With one hand on the door and one on its frame, Hank leaned back and then rocketed out his foot, the flat metal plate that had kept him stuck to his base for so long. It connected with the side of Nichi's chest, just below her arm. The force sent her across the bucket seats and blew the passenger-side door off, leaving Nichi laying in the mud. She gasped for air, but it was no use. Her lungs were both punctured and would never be capable of breathing again.

Hank stepped around the front of the vehicle and stood over her.

A bullet plugged into the front of the van, fired from Parker in a last-ditch attempt to stop the robot. He had leaned himself up against the wall of the motel and sat, pointing the gun at Hank.

"I'll kill you, motherfucker!" he yelled.

Hank paid him no mind. Instead he stood above the woman, rolled her onto her back, and dropped down onto her chest, pressing what was left of her already liquefied insides out through her mouth. But before the lights went out completely, Hank dug his metal thumbs into her mouth, pushing past all the bile, blood, and gunk, and ripped the woman's cheeks off, leaving her with an eternal grin.

Parker fired the last few bullets, none of which hit Hank, as the metal man walked toward him. Hank did nothing to avoid being hit; the man just had shitty aim.

Hank stood over Parker, who continued to pull the trigger to no effect.

"You ain't shit," Parker said, spitting up at him.

Hank reached down and grabbed him by the shirt, lifting him like he was nothing.

"Just fucking do it, man," Parker said.

And Hank did. He pressed his open hand against the man's stomach, shoving him back up against the wall of the motel. Skin and flesh gave way to blood and entrails. The mess ran down Parker's jeans. Hank held him for a moment and then tossed him aside, keeping a handful of what was inside him in one metal palm.

Hank looked down at the gore in his hand, and the line of intestine that led to the man now lying face down in the mud, and unceremoniously dropped it.

The rain had stopped. It was dark, but the sky began to clear.

Hank went to the truck and carefully removed Jillian. He was gentle with her, as he wasn't certain that the dead couldn't still feel. He carried her out into the desert and laid her next to Sandy's grave, where she had buried Albert. He set out to dig, his big metal hands acting as excellent excavators. Once the hole was big enough, he lowered her in and started to cover her with mud. Ratchet supervised, watching every move, ready to let the big fella know if he messed up. When he was finished he pulled two boards from the picnic table and fashioned a cross to mark her grave.

Then Hank set out to walk in the direction all the bad people had come from. If there were survivors out there, and they were like that, Hank had the intention of helping them along their path to the end. Finishing ridding the planet of them after whatever war there had been. He didn't know what he would find, but he was determined to kill it when he found it.

Hank looked back at Ratchet, who sniffed at the newly placed cross. Hank wished he could whistle, but instead he did something else he had seen both Albert and

Jillian, as well as thousands of travelers over the years, do. He patted his thigh with one hand.

Ratchet looked up, started walking toward him, then stopped. The dog looked back at the grave, then to Hank. Hank tapped his leg again.

The dog went back.

Ratchet circled the grave a few times and then lay down in the mud, bathing in the moonlight.

Hank looked toward the hill he'd seen so many cars come over. He had spent his entire existence wondering what lay over that hill. He had changed. He had seen more of the horrors of humanity in the last few hours than he had in all his years prior, and he had earned his title, Sir Hank of Jank, and now the world stood in front of him.

Hank sat in the mud, legs crossed, and Ratchet sat in his lap, getting scratches behind the ear, the way Jillian had always done it. He sat there next to the graves of the only two friends he'd ever known and watched his very first sunrise as a plume of dust came over the hill behind him.

About the Author

Kalvin Ellis is a nice guy who likes stuff. He's online. You should look him up.

Kalvin Ellis

FAN CLUB!

Want to show the gang at school you're rad?!
Join the Kal-vation Army and get a cool surprise!
Get your parents to help you cut out the coupon below and
return it to:

Kalvin Ellis
PO BOX 351501
Westminster CO 80035

Name: _____

Address:_____

City:_____

State:_____Zip:_____

Email (optional for newsletter):_____

Favorite story?

☐ Scissors: A Love Story   ☐ Bury My Body Somewhere Nice
☐ Soft, Chewy Center   ☐ Atomic Despair
☐ In the Dark We Sin

Valid for US Residents. Limited time and while supplies last.
Why not fuck around and find out?

Listed just below will be a group of things that you can expect from most or all of the stories. Specific warnings for each story will be listed directly under that.

General Content Warnings:
Blood, Gore, Bones, Death, Violence, Adult language, Murder

Scissors: A Love Story:
Abusive relationship

Soft, Chewy Center:
Scientific testing on animals, Scientific testing on humans, Claustrophobia

In the Dark We Sin:
Drowning, Police brutality

Bury My Body Somewhere Nice:
Mention of attempted coercion of a minor, Mention of possible sexual assault

Atomic Despair:
Mention of animal dying